Everything in My World Has Been

Paused.

Nothing moves except my heart

It leaps out of my room into the sky

Hangs just above the earth's orbit

It is not alone

He is out there too

He is out there too . . .

GIRLS LIKE ME

by

LOLA StVIL

HOUGHTON MIFFLIN HARCOURT
Boston   New York

This book is for my family:
Ricaldo "I'm okay with takeout—again" Cherubin,
Cindy "The wheels are in motion" St. Vil,
Arnold "How much is this going to cost me?" St. Vil,
And most important, my mom,
Marie "Did you eat?" St. Vil.
I love you.

hmhco.com

The text was set in Amasis MT Std.

The Library of Congress has cataloged the hardcover edition as follows:
Names: StVil, Lola, author.
Title: Girls like me / written by Lola StVil.
Description: Boston : Houghton Mifflin Harcourt, 2016. | Summary: Fifteen-year-
old Shay is trying to cope with being overweight and getting bullied in school, but
when she falls in love with mysterious Blake, insecure Shay needs the help of her
two best friends to make love prevail.
Identifiers: LCCN 2015033387
Subjects: | CYAC: Novels in verse. | Self-esteem—Fiction. | Bullying—Fiction. |
Love—Fiction. | Friendship—Fiction. | Humorous stories. | BISAC: JUVENILE
FICTION / Stories in Verse. | JUVENILE FICTION / Love & Romance. |
JUVENILE FICTION / Humorous Stories. | JUVENILE FICTION / Social Issues
/ Bullying. | JUVENILE FICTION / Girls & Women. | JUVENILE FICTION /
Social Issues / Adolescence.
Classification: LCC PZ7.5.S78 Gi 2016 | DDC [Fic]—dc23 LC record available at
http://lccn.loc.gov/2015033387

ISBN: 978-0-544-70674-3 hardcover
ISBN: 978-1-328-90102-6 paperback

Printed in the United States of America
DOC 10 9 8 7 6 5 4 3 2 1
4500709209

O! be some other name:
What's in a name? that which we call a rose
By any other name would smell as sweet.
—*Romeo and Juliet*

Aftermath

I whip out fake smile reserved for
Monday mornings, cheerleaders
Stepmoms
Kara stitches series of mom-esque words
Forming dubious praise

"Your face is so pretty this morning"
= You *look* fat

"I made egg white omelets and wheat toast"
= So you will no longer *be* fat

"It's nice out. You should walk home today."
= So you can be *less* fat

Kara is stuck
With me
Shay Summers: pretty-faced fat girl who
Reads. Writes. Thinks.
Too much

Dad died
Selfish, Dad, very selfish.

"Don't be late for school"
= Don't stay behind, pig out, get *more* fat

Flashes her best fake smile
The one she keeps in the freezer
So that it stays
Frozen
In
Place

"See you later"

Finally alone, I call on my friends:
Breakfast burrito. Banana cream pie. Butter.

They are all missing
There's been a massacre

Kara's soldiers:
Fat-free
Sugar-free
Reduced
Lite
Skim

Wiped out all my friends
Not even condiments
Remain

I recall
My love

Could it survive savage, unprovoked attack?
Scour area
Attempt rescue

No survivors
Rest in peace,
Apple-wood bacon

Flash of red packaging
Resembles my lover's face

A prayer
A hope
Fragile but real

Pull in closer
Oscar Mayer Bacon!
Turkey bacon?
All is lost . . .

Betrayed
By the time I got to school I was
Fully enraged
I plotted various ways to get rid of Kara
Ways that were
Painful. Slow. Public.
Met up with my best friends

Dash and Boots.
Told them about
Horrific event
Expecting
Outrage. Anger. Protest.

     M
        A
           R
              C
                 H
                    E
                      S

Hell no, we won't go! Hell no, we won't go!
Followed by roar of rebels
Determined not to be subdued by
Fascist taste-free establishment!

Um . . . I kind of like turkey bacon
Dash is right; you should try it
And the (fat-free) cheese
Stands . . . alone.

And Here They Are
Meet the traitors
I mean my friends.

D   A   S   H
And I became best friends in a matter of minutes
Two years ago
First day of school at
Chester A. Arthur High.
He walked into homeroom wearing a
Bedazzled T-shirt that said
I'm not gay but my blow-up doll is.
He was sent to the principal's office

I would share
Similar fate
When
Teacher made us
Sit in
ABC order.
Shay Summers sits next to arch nemesis
Kelly Stokes

K   E   L   L   Y
Is what happens when Beauty sleeps with
Empty
We went to the same junior high.
At face value
Her face had
Value

Her eyes, cobalt-blue orbs of
Perfect
Her lips, heart-shaped
Masterpiece
Her skin, flawless
Radiance.
But Kelly was a road trip to the
Grand Canyon
No matter how much it promises to
Enchant. Amaze. Delight.
Once you get there
You realize
It's just an empty hole

She never says anything that doesn't come out of
Teen Cosmo
Popsugar.com
Never reads anything that doesn't have
Super-high-gloss finish
And
I'm fairly certain her ego has its own
Orbit
Enough, Shay
Make an effort
Jump into the chasm . . .

Why?
Maybe she was
Miss Understood
Cool Chick
Deep Deep Deep
D
O
W
N???

So I Smiled
Turns out deep down
Is not that deep
After all
Kelly looks at me
Like I'm a hobo
Trying to pee on her
I have done the unthinkable
She mumbles loud enough for

E   V   E   R   Y   O   N   E
On the
P   L   A   N   E   T
To hear
"Quick, get up, Shay! The chair can only hold
A ton"

Rage Bubbled

Up from throat
Prepared to erupt and melt the smug flesh off her
Perfectly sculpted bones
Prepared a litany of profanity that would make any
Truckers. Sailors. Mobsters.
Proud
I SHOUTED
"The Grand Canyon is just a hole!"
What???????
Where's the alphabet soup
Of curses?
The string of profanity that's supposed to wrap
Itself around her neck till she turns
Blue?

The Only Color in the World Now

Is tomato red
Spreading across my cheeks
Hands
Are frozen
Shaking
Shivering
No control over breathing
Can't find rock to crawl under
The teacher sent me
To the principal's office.

There I found
Dash waiting also
He was scribbling doodles and letters on scrap paper
I admired his *M*
It could have come out of a penmanship workbook.
Except he added more loops than were needed
He said, "That's me: more loops than needed."
I told him about my run-in with
Kelly Canyon
The principal/chef
Served us two boilerplates of
What-we-expect-from-our-students
I had a side of glazed
How-a-lady-should-act
And Dash had the stuffed
We-will-not-tolerate-tomfoolery
For dessert we both had the caramelized
Next-time-I-will-call-your-parents
Next morning, Canyon
Found a magazine cutout of a model
Taped to her locker
Someone had made an air bubble above the model's head
It said *Feed Me*
The *M* had an extra loop
Like I said
Friends for life.

My Other Best Friend

And I met at the nurse's office
When I was there to avoid
Gym
I am the CEO of
Getting Out of Class Inc.
My excuses are
Prompt. Polished. Perfect.
And what's more
I have amazing range
I'm not like your average
Teen going AWOL
I don't kill off
Grandmothers or get cramps
My excuses come complete with
Actors. Script revisions. Dress rehearsals.
That day I was faking stomach pains
Had full written menu
Of all things that could have caused my
Pain
I did the well-rehearsed "brave face" so that they knew
how much
I really wanted to stay in gym class.
The "suffer in silence face"
Is the meatloaf and mashed potatoes of excuses
I saw her as soon as I entered
She was beautiful. Beaming. Bald.
She wore

"Army" everything, including
Combat boots
> "Punk rocker cool?" I asked.
>
> "Brain tumor chic," she said.

I looked around for a rock to crawl under
To hide shame
With no rock to be found anywhere
I sat a few chairs away from her
In my head
> I played every sad song
>
> I ever heard in the
>
> Someone-I-love-is-dying
>
> Movie
>
> Genre

She stopped my soundtrack
"Don't do the sympathy head tilt," she said.
"How about the I'm-pulling-for-you shoulder pat?" I asked.
"No thanks," she replied.
> She asked what I was in for
>
> "Shamelessness," I admitted.
>
> "Faking it? Yeah, me too," she lied.
>
> A smile slid onto my face
>
> Then I met her eyes

She wasn't joking
The tumor gave her
Headaches
She spoke casually about it
As if she was just asked about the time

Damn
I offered her my finest *I'm so sorry* face
But something told me she wouldn't take it
Pity clashes with her kick-ass boots

The Three of Us
Have never figured out how to
Fit
Into the puzzle
Of
High school
We suck
At being like
Others
And while we
Hardly understand
Self
It's all we know

Homeroom
Is where I sit and carve short strokes
On my desk
Like prisoners do on walls
Or
Do math homework I didn't do the night before.

The teacher tells us what she thinks we need to know:
Upcoming
Trips. Fire drills. Tests.
She skips what we actually want to hear:
There
Is
No
Class today.
(A girl can dream.)

While I do
Homework
That
Should
Have
Been
Done
Night
Before
I invite you, take a tour
Inside
Minds
Of the student body . . .
AKA:
The White Noise

The Troublemaker
They can tell I'm wearing the same jeans
Again
Punch. Push. Pound.
Sent off to principal's office
Suspension: one week
Good
Old jeans will be
New again

Head of Audio-Visual
Chess Club
Glee Club
No-One-
Likes-Me
Club
Gonna get good grades
Lead to great job. Make mad money.
And buy everyone

Afterschool Helper
Make copies. Stock books. Clean board.
It's late. "Go home," she says.
Smile. Don't panic.
"Just a few more copies to make," I lie.
"Okay," she says.

Relief fills lungs
Can't go home
Can't go home

Head Cheerleader

They love me.
Love.
Me?
When?
Since teeth bleached, hair dyed
I died.
Hours hunting hot trends
Duties include but not limited to
Spirit crushing. Ball busting. Soul sucking.
Others.
Merely playing the role I was cast in by
Mom
Request script change
New words, same thoughts

Something peeks out: more words
Squatting, hiding behind other words
Yank them from behind, lay them out before my mirror
I am so lonely, I could die

Teacher's Pet
Oh, oh, me, me!
Pick me! Pick me! Me!
I am her eyes in her absence
I want to do it. I need to do it. I have to do it.
Power. Ah, yes. Thank you.
Um . . . how do you do this?

Freak
Ink me.
Dragons. Demons. Blades.

Call me.
Freak. Crazy. Psycho.

See me.
Handle. Labels. Easy.

Why not?
Damage? Raid? Destroy?

My home:
Steady. Solid. Safe.

Been taught:
Love
Is only
Label that
Matters

The Slacker
They say I am not working hard enough.
I got dressed. Got on the bus, knowing it was headed for
     school.
My work is done.
Anyway, no one expects much.

Security Guard
Hey, kid, you look down. Need a pick-me-up? First fix free . . .

Five-Finger Discount
It's not a cry for help; it's just the only thing
I'm good at

Coach
That kid's good, almost as good as I was.
Back when I . . . was

Teacher

She's late. Again. Bet she doesn't have her assignment.

I knew it!

He's got the answers, the scores, and the aptitude

Won't get girls, though!

New kid looks high . . .

I'm low

On yellow and blue pills

Wonder who his supplier is . . .

Bookworm in the corner

She needs to apply lip gloss or

Prep for life of cats, ratty sweaters, and can of soup for one

Oh, look who didn't cut class today

Guess all the girls have been deflowered

Lucky his dad's got old money and new cars

Principal

Love kids

Taught them for years

Promoted. Promoted. Principal.

Handle

~~Kids~~

Paperwork

That's Not Everyone

But I have to get going
I have to navigate the crowded halls and get to history class
History: Someone did something back then
And we're forced to
Act like it matters now.

In a Blur of Facts and Dates

History passes by
Head to science
Mr. Todd has never had a student say anything
Bad about him, but we keep expecting to see him on those
Predators-caught-on-tape shows
His episode would start when he
Arranges to meet a minor
Greets her with
Candy. Six-pack. Hard-on.
He looks like
Mr. Rogers
But the way he fondles the
Molecule orb sculptures on his desk
While licking his lips . . .
Makes me glad I don't live in his neighborhood.

English Class Actually Doesn't Suck

Putting together a story or reading some great American
    classic
Is almost as good as pie
To think a story could be written so well that it
Captivated the world, and is still being read centuries later.
Awesome.

I wonder if what I have written will last that long.
Doubt it. A hundred years from now who will want to know
    that
Kara sucks? Kelly Canyon is evil? And
Shay Summers misses her dad's
Bass-filled laugh
Knock-knock jokes
      I
A   R
Guitar?
She misses them
So much she can hardly breathe . . .

Still

If I am to become a writer most revered
I guess I better step up my work
Then again, I'm sure Shakespeare would not have spent his
    whole time

Writing *Romeo and Juliet* if he had had a cell phone
He'd just text the story and it would get forwarded to
All his friends

Incoming text from William S.
yng luv c-ks 2 bl@hsum @Mung sAvG
vyl3ns & d!scrd. <3rs r34uZn 2 b
Prtd, 4loh thAr
H@rtz on2 a tR@gC fA+3
(Young love seeks to blossom among savage
Violence and discord. Lovers, refusing to be parted, follow their
Hearts on to a tragic fate)

I Was Headed to Lunch When I Saw the Poster
With innocent letters gathered on page
To form a profane phrase: *Halloween DANCE*
Word spreads. Excitement builds.
Only question asked:
Who asked you to the dance?
A question no one will ask me, certain
No one has asked me
Busy anyway
Books to redevour
DVDs to rewatch
Tiles to recount
Solitaire to play

Stupid. Cruel. Useless. Letters. Forming
words to spite me.
Longing to shout, "I am going to the
dance with Blake."

Blake Harrison: God.

Master. King. Sultan.

Of all things hot. Cool. Sextastic.

Able to render me

Motionless. Mute. Mortified.

(If caught stealing a glance)

He walks freely inside the pages of

Textbooks. Notebooks. Journals.

Rescues me without

Super strength. Cape. Theme song.

Simply with his

Walk. Smile. Eyes.

So . . .

Shock! Defy! Announce!

Blake Harrison, my date.

Yes, it would be a lie.

Still . . .

It's a pretty lie.

It sparkles when the light hits it just right

See there?

Right there, it gleams
My lie: more valuable than
Their truth
Their truth: ugly
Cold. Jagged. Rocks.
Cutting into me, making me bleed
But my lie?
She is a gift. A gift so beautiful
Must be allowed to live!
The lie dances out of my soul
And charges into their world
Blake Harrison asked me to the dance!

Lie leaps into air, bounces off walls, slides down doors
Falls flat on ground.
No one reaches to save her.
No one hears her cry out
Run over, pick her up
She's bruised. Broken.
She's dull now
Even in my light
Kelly Canyon walked by
The disappointment on my face warmed her
Like Mama's apple pie

How Did the Canyon Come to Be

My mortal enemy?
It all came down to chocolate milk
Lawson McGee had
Red hair. Green eyes. Great smile.
And
Extra chocolate milk
At age twenty
Jewelry says: love
At five, it's chocolate milk
Lawson McGee handed
It to me and not Kelly
Since then I have been
On her radar

I mostly avoid her
But like any demon she has
Powers
A swarm of dark birds
Descend
Notifying her that I'm feeling
Crappy

Kelly Is

     Pimple on prom night
Kelly is
     Text message to wrong person
Kelly is
     Period. Blood. White skirt.
Dread in its true form

She Leaves Me Gifts

Stuffed pig with built-in
"Oink"
In my locker
On my chair
In my backpack

How Do I Thank Her?

Tears. Tears. Tears.
Surely she's tired of getting my
Thank-you cards

It's Said That

She and Blake belong
Together
Gods and goddesses
Often do
Yet Zeus
Seeks only a passing friendship
With her sound and fury
Preferring the company of cool breezes

A Moment

After she embarrasses
Me
A moment
After she destroys
Me
On her face there
L   I   V   E   S
Utter peace

Kelly Acted Like a Person One Day

Someone died, someone she loved
Grandmother
I think
Kelly
Looked small

Shrinking Inside
I gave her a gift by
Walking by
Inhaling food
She
Made rude comment
She got
B   I   G   G   E   R
And
I began to fade

The Day

Is half over. Thankfully. I have been trying to
Stay cool and avoid
Dash and Boots
As soon as they remember
What tomorrow is, they'll
Worry

    I may break down
    They'll text throughout the day
    Asking stupid but vital questions
    Best friends have to ask
Are you ok? they'll say.
Tomorrow is one-year anniversary
Of my dad's death, and since he's still
Dead, I am not okay.

At Lunch

I take the path less traveled to get to the cafeteria
(They knew I would)
They wait for me by the door
I smile
Too much.
I look like a walking Crest commercial
"Girl, you know you have to talk to us," Dash says
Boots looks at me with sadness.
         "Boots, you know the rules: Only tumor girls get
         Sympathy head tilts. The rest of us
            get hard candy
         And five-dollar gift cards to iTunes,"
           I remind her.
We sit at the table
I say that I'm fine even before they ask
Dash hands me his prized possession:
Embroidered handkerchief with the names of every
Project Runway winner
Since Season One
I burst into tears
I hate that they know me so well . . .

Once the Tears Came

Getting them to stop?
Impossible

I missed rest of my classes, huddled up in the girls' bath-
    room
Until the bell rang, then off to the library
                    The school library
                    Has been my friend since *The Cat in the*
                            Hat
I wanted to jump inside each and every book when I was a
    kid
Dad said if I was good he'd let me jump
Into *Green Eggs and Ham*
When I turned five, he gave me a
Green Eggs and Ham party
Including green eggs and ham
                    The librarian knows me by name
                    I spend lots of time in here
                    Too much, Dash says
The library was near empty
The quiet life-saving.

The Quiet

Was still so loud inside my head
I replayed the day I found out my dad died
I wanted to stop the film in the beginning
'Cause I knew how it ended . . .

The News

That Dad died came
From a telephone call from Kara
I hate it when she calls me
I almost didn't pick up
Why, oh why, didn't I send her
To voicemail?

She Told Me

To come home ASAP
I thought we were in for another bonding night
I looked for
Rope. Arsenic. Knife.
Something, anything, to end my life.
I had lived fourteen years; that was enough.
Could not handle any more bonding
No court in the world would force me to
Hang with
K A R A
Smiled as she worked out
Called everyone "sweetie"
Put a line through her 7s
Like the French do.
So, the good old USA
Was not good
Enough for her

She was an awful woman.
Yet something in her voice
A quiet sob? A shaking?

Once Home
I felt something was off
Everything looked the same but something had changed
No, they found out I'm about to fail
Math
Damn it!
Entered kitchen, found her
Sitting in corner, crying
Please, please, let it be about math . . .
Although
She had borrowed
A handful of words from neighbors
And placed them at my feet
Car. Speed. Head.
Docs. Tried. Dad. Dead.

SCREW HER!!!
For placing these lies near me
I'm calling Dad
He'll fix everything.

I Threw Things
At Kara
I
Swore. Begged. Cried.
She would not
Take words back.
Dad would not
Pick up cell.
Everyone
Failed me

How Could He Leave Me?
We had plans
Plays. Movies. Concerts.
He said he'd help me with
Math. Science. Life.
I could just kill him

What Did I Do?

What words did I

S   T   R   I   N   G
    O
    G
    E
    T
    H
    E
    R

That made him go away?
Crying is pointless
'Cause it won't bring him back
And that makes me cry . . .

The Sun Came

Up in the
East
Down in the
West
The clock
Ticked
The clock
Tocked
The mailman
Brought
Us

33

Mail
Man . . .
Guess they don't know
He's gone.

Dad's Funeral Happened

The same day as my favorite
TV show.
I went up to my room to catch it and
Escape the chorus of
"I'm so sorry for your loss"
"He was a good man"
"He will always be with you"
She came to
MY ROOM. Said
I was being rude
Excuse me for having skipped
The "etiquette" chapter of grieving.
She thought I was being mean
I was
That's what happens when half of you
Is underground

The Next Few Days

Kara and I
Held on to each other

She made me tea. Her hands were too shaky to pour.
The water grew cold. Eventually so did things
Between us.
When Dad was alive he
Measured. Mixed. Marinated.
Like a chef
(In *his*
Mind)
ACTUALLY
Everything Dad made: burned
Then Kara came
Offered to cook all the things
We SHOULD like
She changed him
His marriage changed me
I
Became
TEEN MONSTER
She became
TEEN MONSTER SLAYER
He became
PEACEMAKER
Had a picture in her head
Of what family would be like
My family, her head
She pictured me
Thinner
I pictured her

Gone
      Dad made olive branches
      For us to extend to each other
      Instituted (mandatory)
      Movie Night. Game Night. Girls' Night.
All
      Hell Night
At first, Dad's death made: bridge
But time reveals truth: Kara and I are
Strangers with
Different pictures of what happy looks like
She hates that I am not hers
I hate that she is not mine
Dad
Measured. Mixed. Marinated.
Like a chef
Everything Dad made: burned
Dad's death made: bridge
Everything Dad made:
Burned . . .

They Find Me

Dash and Boots
I knew they would
They try to cheer me up
With dirty joke about hookers
Peanut butter and rope

I wonder what would happen
If they put their imaginations to
Good productive use
They want to hang
Just to have fun, they say
Really it is to keep an eye on
Me
They worry I will
Feel lonely and bad again
If left to myself
Truth is I have been
Lonely in
Crowds
Lonely
In the middle
Of conversations
There is no
Escape
Tomorrow will come
And so will
The blues
Dash makes one last
Plea.
Says we can go to revival of
The Rocky Horror Picture Show
He wants us to come with
So he can have someone's hand to squeeze
When the beauty of

Tim Curry is too much to bear
Boots says she will go
Only if free large popcorn w/drink
Is involved
Friendship comes at a price
And today it's $9.50

Boots Reminds Me

I promised I would check out Firetrash.com
A site originally created by nerd lovers from our school
But is now flooded with non-Trekkies
Boots stays on there for hours
Discussing important subjects
Does Stewie have a crush on Brian?
Has Gene Roddenberry's dream
Been *fully* realized?
And where, oh where, can she find
The Rocky Horror Picture Show
On Blu-ray?
I only said I would go there because she held my burrito
Hostage last week.
Because of my love for
All things sour cream and cheesy
I have to go online and
Face the White Noise
She promises she will be online later and we can talk
I point out that we can also pick up a phone

Dash adds that I am the only person on the planet
Who does not have a Facebook account

Facebook
A public record of all the friends
I don't have . . .

I Agree
To check it out
Easier
Than arguing
  She says it has everything:
  411 on best tattoo places
  Deals on sci-fi gear
  Total access to all things *Lost*
    I could have pointed out that
    Lost is off the air
    But that's like pointing out
    Edward Cullen is a killer
    Sookie and Bill Compton don't belong together
    Elvis is not coming back
    Some people cannot process
    The truth, and hell
    Why should they have to?
    Truth takes apart
    Everything in its path

As I Make My Way Home

A grayness crawls from the soles
Of my feet
Slides up my legs, thighs, stomach, and chest
Think of something
Chase it away
How? How?
Ben & Jerry's just up the block.
Salvation . . .

There Is God

In ice cream
Don't let anyone tell you different
Americone Dream. Chunky Monkey. Cherry Garcia.
Heaven in three scoops
How can something so divine
Be right here on earth?
Don't question
Eat. Eat. Eat.
Till nothing hurts
After heaven everything else
Is hell (AKA home)

Home

Is a minefield
I avoid hot spots, try and make it to my room

First scurry past kitchen
Where Kara watches healthy cooking show
Run past Dad's bedroom
Fight the urge to peek in and call out his name
Still think he's in there somewhere . . .
Rush past hallway closet where
His running sneakers sit foolishly
Waiting for him

Some Days
I can make it past every trap and enter my room
A whole girl
Some Days
A sharp pain rips me from the inside: I make it to my room
In pieces
Some Days
I have to close my eyes so I won't see all the places he used to
Exist
Some Days
I can't take my eyes off the last things he
Touched
Some Days
I rage against his ghost for not going away
Some Days
I weep at the thought that his ghost might fade

Consolation

Comes in the form of a greasy
Brown bag
I carry
Into room
I demolished
Cheesy. Double-decker. Goodness.
Then had the eleven herbs and spices from the colonel
In case you wondered
Loneliness resides at the bottom of a KFC bucket

Homework

Just won't be done today
Good thing I don't have my sights set on good schools
I'm thinking of going to a party school
That way my "half in" and "half out" approach to
Learning will be appreciated

There's a Knock on the Door

It's Kara
She says something about dinner
I say no.
She asks what I've had to eat
"Carrots and tofu," I lie
She is not amused

She says she made veggies and skinless chicken
Seriously?

A Promise

To a friend can't be taken lightly
I said I would go on Firetrash.com
And I will, but I never said how long
I would stay on there
So, one click, one glance
And I am done.

Firetrash.com

Is a site where hundreds of kids
From school feast on judgment and ridicule
A meal I refuse to take part in

I Am About To

Log off when I spot a chatroom with
Only one member
His profile says that he is male
The odd thing is he keeps typing as if
Talking to someone
     The username is Godotwait4me
     And he is in the middle of talking about his day:

Forced to mow lawn clean out garage
Pretend to care about sports
It's all so . . .
Exhausting.

On a Whim

I answer back and agree to send him
A kit filled with fake smiles
Convincing head nods, and jelly beans

This Is Stupid

He won't get the joke. See?
No reply. Whatever
Suddenly
Words appear . . .
> **Godotwait4me says:**
> Can I get Jolly Ranchers instead?
Sorry, no substitutions, I reply
Lol. I like you already
I bet you say that to all the fonts that appear on your screen
You caught me. You a girl?
I don't giggle, braid hair, or own anything pink, but yes
And here I am, desperately in need of a giggling/hair
    braiding/girl with a pink tee
Why Godot?
It's a play

I know. I read it. A play about a guy who never shows up

You read? Sexy

That's what my teachers had in mind when they were
    teaching me—get her all sexed up!

And your user name—notall2gether

It's not that deep

No. btw neither am I

You an old guy?

Why? Walkers turn you on?

Along with the old man smell

I'm 15. But 16 promises to come along soon

Same here but I'm growing doubtful

Why? 15 killing you?

Slowly . . .

OK, lets make a deal. Whichever one of us spots 16 first
    vows to beat it down and hold it hostage

Deal. Who were you talking to on here?

No one

Why?

"No one" always takes my side

Mine too

Gotta go. Sister needs to get online. See if the outfit she
    bought 5 seconds ago is still in style

K, bye

I'm hurt

Why?

No request for further contact? Was my sentence structure
    not romantic enough?

45

Um . . . no, you form sentences like a gentleman.
So . . . give me your address. I'll email.
Um, no you won't
I'm sorry madam but your crystal ball is in need of repair
Did you say madam?
Um . . . no? Typo. I am cool, hip guy who would never say
    such a thing
Here's the info
Thx, ttyl
Really?
Really

What Was That?
He wanted my info
Um . . .
That's cool
Whatever.
No big deal.
Oh no, how do I do that thing again?
Oh yeah: inhale, exhale (repeat)

She Says
Don't read this email
That I'm sending only minutes after we talked.
He's reading it!

Damn.

We need an opening

So . . . come here oft—

No, not that.

Nice weather we're hav—

No!

How 'bout those Yankees?

You're kidding, right?

Okay, move on.

Entice him with

Your

Eyes

iiiiiiiiiiiiiiiiiiiiiiiiiiiiiiiiiiiiiiiiiiiiiiiiiiiiiiiiiiiiiiiiiiiiiiiiiiiiiiiiiiiiiii

No!

I mean your e-y-e-s!

Oh, forget it.

He's losing interest.

Quick!

Show some leg.

Not that much

Do you want him to think you're

Easy?

Never mind; just flash him a smile

: -))

Now that's just cheesy

Hurry!

He's moving on

Say something
Sexy
That will
Linger
In his mind
Redrum
SEXY, NOT SCARY!
Oh, just forget it!

He Won't Email Me Back

Should not have sent it
Let things fade to black

I Was Wrong

He replies:
Impress her
Use big words
Dromiceiomimus
Dinosaurs?
I said impress
Not bore.

Say something that would come out of one of those
Black-and-white chick flicks
Where everyone

Smokes
Hey, throat cancer, anyone?
What!
Who says that?
It's the truth!
Tell her she is nice.
That seems kind of obvious.
Tell her she's articulate
Again, kind of obvious.
Tell her she's been on your mind
Since her first post.
She doesn't really need to know th —

Hey! Who pressed send!!!

She Says
Everything you were told to run from, run to
I gave my last sexy smile to a homeless guy
Who hadn't smiled in days
Now I've nothing to lure you with

Yesterday, I tripped
All my charm cracked open
Spilled out onto the sidewalk
Now I have no way to distract you from my shortcomings

I spent my last buck
On a sock full of holes
Cast out by the other socks
Now, I can't afford *Teen Mag*
So I'll never know
How to hook him with one look

Still . . .
I send this out
In hopes that you have a thing for smileless
Charmless, broke girls.

He Says
Reveal!
Who told you about my
Secret
Passion
For
Broke/charmless/smileless girls?
No one is supposed to know
Is
Nothing
Sacred?

She Says
The night we didn't spend

I'll list everything I'm looking for
And, wait! It's what you're
Looking for too (wow)

We'll send emails
About stupid things we don't
Really care about (um . . . yeah, it was really cold today)

You'll want a
Picture
Just in case I'm ugly

I'll want a picture
Just in case I'm
Not as open-minded as I let on
(Man, look at his ears)

The emails will
Get shorter
You'll forget why you wrote to me

I'll forget why I
Responded

I'll watch a movie by myself and pretend I'm
The girl in
The flick with the two-inch waistline and the newly shined
Happy ending
(Courtesy of MGM)

You'll go to a concert and pretend
You're one of those
Guys who got dragged there by friends
You'll meet girls whose names you won't remember
(Jessica, Jenny? Oh, yeah
Rachel)

I will turn off the TV just in time to hear the neighbors
Fight.
She forgot his birthday. He never holds her anymore.
I will think maybe it's good
I'm alone.

Then he tells her the game is on.
She will say, So?
He will say, So . . . let's go in the bedroom and turn it off

They
Turn it off
All night

And I will think maybe alone isn't so good.

You will hear a couple fighting
She flirts too much. He
Never pays her any mind.

You will think maybe it's better I'm alone.
He
Gets mad and walks off.
She
Runs after him and falls
He rushes to her side
Comforts and kisses her

You will think
Maybe alone is not so
Good.

I will think
Me too

You will walk home—alone
Me too

You will go online
Start all over again
Me too

'Cause neither one of us wants to spend a night
Like the night we didn't spend

He Says

Can't keep
Smile away from
Lips
You away from
Thoughts

She Says

New days of the week
She didn't want to reply to him
But epic poems
Period dramas
Cell phone ads
All
Promised
Love
Just around the corner

She looked; it wasn't
Maybe
     She
            Should
               Change
The menu.
Add a hot item
Sex pie w/whip cream on the side
But then

He'd only
Come
For the food
Besides
She wasn't ready to
"Cook"

She wanted to count
Days
Days not written
On calendars

He-convinces-me-I'm-not-a-dork Mondays
Our-sides-hurt-from-laughter-after-tasting Tuesdays
The-school's-loose-interpretation-of-meatloaf Wednesdays
We're-holding-hands-and-gravity-no-longer-works-on-me
        Fridays
I-
Called-
Just-
To-hear-
Your-
Voice
Sundays.

But she hasn't found him
So weekdays are just
Weekdays

She didn't want to reply
But epic poems
Period dramas
Cell phone ads
All
Promised
Love
Just around the corner . . .

He Says/She Says
This morning
Everything
Is still
It's like they know
What today is
The washing machine
Churned
The toaster
Popped
The radio
Sang
All
Trying
To convince
Me
Things were
Normal

Normal was something Dad wasn't
Always good at

As we say our goodbyes
Alarm sounds
Cell sends me
Daily reminder from
Dad

A quick "parent" text that held
No value
At the time
But now means
Everything

Honey, remember
No homework, no concert
Love, Dad

I saved his message
And reread it every night
As if that could
Keep him here with me . . .

Like When I Was Six

Dad forced a road trip on me
The thought of spending hours

In a metal box w/my dad
Made me want to die
How many hours of
News radio would I be
Subjected to?
I
Begged. Cried. Pleaded.
Threatened
To
        Hold
            My
                Breath

Dad said
Blue looked
Good
On me

When he got in the car
My real dad stayed back at home
This new dad was
Someone else
Someone
Who
Sang along w/the radio
Tapped along with the beat on the steering wheel
And

Whistled
My dad
Whistled!

I had never heard the songs
That were playing
He said it was a crime not to know them
So he set out to teach me
Hours and hours of old-people tunes
He played them over
And over again
After a while
They didn't
Suck

Every pit stop
That had an interesting
Window display
We'd pull over and
Explore
Pick up
Essential things:
Stuffed pink alligator
Glitter-laced yarn
Bejeweled box of
Pop-Tarts

And
Corn dogs
Lots of
Corn dogs

By the time we got back
I had
Tummy ache
Nausea
Body ache

In school
We were asked to
Get up and talk about what we did
That weekend

I didn't talk
I sang
And according to my teacher
I was the only six-year-old in the world
Who knew all the lyrics to
"American Pie"
In other words
I
Rule!

Mom Would

Get bored
Easily

            Even
            Microwave
            Wait was
            Too long

We would
Laugh
At what she left behind:
Frozen dinners. Cold coffee. Stale popcorn.

Then she started leaving
Bigger things:
Home. Dad. Me.

Searched My Memory

To find
Moment
Where
It became
Too much

            Did I
            Cry
            Too much

Eat
Too much
Need
Too much?

Fifteen Years Ago

A woman was
Sentenced
To prison
With
No locks. No gates. No doors.

Yet she could not
Break free
Forced to
Care. Listen. Love.
Every day
Every Day
EVERY DAY

She would plan
Escape
Map out routes to
F R E E D O M

Then she ran
For

> Her life

Because she
Wanted
> Her life

Like it was
Before . . .

Angela Summers's To-Do List:

1. Silence the mommy alarm with cereal
2. Go to balcony (hiding place)
3. Smoke one cigarette while surveying suburbia (prison)
4. Conceal tears with best smile
5. Turn on TV for the parasite (good way to shut her up)
6. Leave snacks on table (faster way to shut her up)
7. Return to bed (repeat until sweet death comes)

"Thank You for Calling the Universe!
This is Ron from Topeka, Kansas
How may I fix your life today?"

> "Hi Ron! I ordered a mom
> Serial number 4836-57-0047
> But the one you sent me

Doesn't work
She's defective."

"Would you like us to send you a new one?"

"No, please send someone to fix the one I have
I'd like to keep her."

"Did you try shutting her down
And rebooting or hard reset?"

"My dad did. Sent her to spa
She came back the same:
Silent. Sad. Sorry."

"She may have a broken motherboard."

"What do I do, Ron?"

"We are all out of the model you have. And we have no
    upgrades.
However, we can send you a shipment of pie along with
    our apologies."

"What can a pie do? Can pie fix this?"

"Pie can fix anything . . ."

I Didn't Cry the First Day
She left
Dad did
A lot

       I knew she would go
       Because she let me have
       Ice cream for dinner
       (A little sweet before the bitter)

Mom was
Movie paused
Midway

       Bird halted
       Midflight

Waterfall frozen
Midstream

I Learned to Arm Myself
From Mom
Dad, though,
Had
No protection
No defense
Against
His wife's absence

       He looked for her
       At first
       He ached for her

At first
He felt for her
At first
Then one day
He made dinner
(Not takeout)
Baked chicken and rice
The chicken had no
Taste
The rice had no
Salt
"How's the food, Shay?"
He asked
"Amazing!"
I lied
He smiled
I smiled
Then we weren't
Trio
Missing
Member
We were
Duo
We
Became
Us . . .

I Would Have Missed Her

And felt unwanted
Had it not been for him
He always made sure we were
Busy
Too
Busy
To be
Sad
Busy learning how to
Make:
Milk come out my nose
Play:
Perfect air guitar
Sing:
All-burp version of "Twinkle, Twinkle, Little Star"
Then Dad went on
Blind date
Her name was
Kara
She liked:
Carrots. Ballet. Yoga.
A   N   D
Breaking up families

Just a Few Short Months

After they met, he proposed
So . . . I "lost" my dad
A year before
I lost my dad
I am no one's child.

What Does One Wear

To visit a grave?
Jeans and turtleneck
Red to match the roses I will bring
The ones he will never smell

Standing in Front of His Grave

My fantasy plays out:
His name is spelled wrong
It's some kind of mystery
I become Sherlock
Solve the case
Discover
It's all been a mistake
He is alive and well. I pore over his headstone
In search of an error
Here lies

Richard D. Summers
Beloved husband and father

Nothing is out of place
Except
Me

On the Way Back Home
Kara asks
What I want to do

Go to Dad's favorite restaurant?
Watch old home movies?
Look through old albums?

Will that bring him back?

Her back stiffens
She bites lower lip and cries
She thinks I shot her with Spiteful Bullet
But that which
Rips through and cuts
Deeply was not born of
Cruelty but of hope

Odd

How
In the same breath
Live two different daughters

I am fully committed
To being angry at him for dying on me
I
Hate
Hate
Hate
Him

I want him back
I need him back
Beyond what words convey

I
Love
Love
Love
Him

Odd
How in the same breath
Live two different daughters

A Gift Basket

Awaits me at the front door. On top is a card written in
Positively perfect penmanship

Could not find sweet, sexy hottie
To send over to you.
So these treats and my love
Will have to do
          —Dash

How Could I

Have given Dash such a blah intro?
He deserves so much more
Let me try again
This time in his own star-studded, jewel-encrusted words
Here is

* * *Dash Montgomery!!!* * *

Dare to be honest

About who you really are

Say you don't care when they reject you

Hope they focus on dazzle of shirt, not tear in eye

To Tell the Truth
I tried, but girl parts are just . . .
GROSS

My Dad
Spends minutes, hours, days searching
Photos, videos, flashbacks
Desperately seeking
The moment that turned me gay
A word spoken.
A gesture made.
A warning missed.
But where . . . ?

He looks for answers
In my

Eyes. Walk. Laugh.
He begs the gods to know why
I am
This way

I Kissed

Joel Martin in the laundry room of his mom's house
His skin was soft and warm
He smelled like April Fresh fabric softener
And grape juice
The washing machine tumbled and rumbled
Thunder in my ears
My skin on his made currents
Travel from spine
To tips of toes
He pulled away
Said boys like me go to hell

I guess it was only right: I had already been
To heaven

Mom and Dad Fight

She says she loves me for me
He says he loves me too
If only . . .

My Love

I bring you home in brown bag
Sneak you to my room
Lock door, pull down shades, jump into bed
Pull covers over me; no one need view my private shame
How can a self-respecting gay kid love
Carburetors
Intake manifolds
Fuel lines?
Want to share my love
With Dad but can't
He'd think he'd found
Hope

My Dad Keeps Trying to Fix Me

Why can't I be broken?

Gambling

Mom brings chips
I bring soda
We vow to bring
Veggies next time
(We vowed that last time)
Heidi Klum is as always
Flawless

Mom says she could look that good
If she worked out more
I say she'd need surgery
She attacks with savage weapon: accent pillows *with
    buttons*
The designers, overwhelmed
Mom and me, overjoyed
The hopefuls create
Extraordinary gowns
We argue over:
Hemlines. Bustlines. Deadlines.
No way he can finish that beadwork in time.
Mom disagrees. We bet. Loser does dishes.
Mom thinks judges will love feather accent
I say no, they won't
We bet. Loser cleans up.

Mom thinks dress is divine
I think it's trash
We bet.
Loser forks over ten bucks.
It's almost midnight
Can't sleep
Have to
Scrub pots. Vacuum floor. Call Shay.
(Hope she has ten bucks)

Looking at Dash's Gift

I know it's only a matter of time before Boots comes by
I'm hoping she won't
I need to get rest
Don't feel like company
I have been able to keep
Tears at bay with
Friends. Food. Fond memories of Dad.
And my secret weapon:
A text from Godot
Or so I hoped . . .

Stupid, Huh?

Well, it's been hours and no text
My weapon has been taken away
With each tick of the clock
I am defenseless

An Hour Into

Drowning in the salty black sea
Of useless tears
My cell sings a song
Letting me know someone has texted . . .

Godotwait4me: You there? Hello?

notall2gether: Um hi

Godotwait4me: What's wrong?

notall2gether: Who said something is wrong?

Godotwait4me: The 3 min pause is a great clue

notall2gether: Oh

Godotwait4me: So . . . what's wrong?

notall2gether: Don't want to talk about it. Want to run from it. Fast and far

Godotwait4me: I can make that happen. Where to?

notall2gether: Chile

Godotwait4me: Why?

notall2gether: What other country's name means both weather and a delicious winter soup?

Godotwait4me: If that's the case, I say we go to Turkey

notall2gether: Anywhere but here

Godotwait4me: Tell me something about you

notall2gether: Like what?

Godotwait4me: Something no one knows

notall2gether: I used to marry my socks

Godotwait4me: ???

notall2gether: When I was 5 I thought each sock needed to venture away from the pair it came with.

notall2gether: It's like they were in an arranged marriage. I felt it was my job to allow them to be with whoever their hearts truly desired

Godotwait4me: So . . . red socks went with pale pink socks?

notall2gether: Red socks could be with blue or yellow socks. I was a very open-minded ruler

Godotwait4me: LMAO. How did you marry them?

notall2gether: Once they found their mate, I would wear the pair to school

Godotwait4me: You wore mismatched socks every day?

notall2gether: Just about

Godotwait4me: Bet you were popular

notall2gether: Yeah the kids called me names

Godotwait4me: What?

notall2gether: Well, I used to love reading out loud and I had the mismatch socks so . . . Reading Rainbow

Godotwait4me: Not laughing

notall2gether: Liar. I can hear you from here

Godotwait4me: Can't type. Rolling on the floor

notall2gether: Hey, I brought a lot of couples together

Godotwait4me: I heard sock couples have the lowest divorce rate in the nation. Good job

notall2gether: I try

Godotwait4me: Too bad you couldn't have worked your magic on my Mom and Dad. They're getting a divorce

notall2gether: Sorry

Godotwait4me: Me too

notall2gether: I have a stepmom. Kara. Keep waiting for her to fall down a flight of stairs

Godotwait4me: You can't just wish for a person's death, Rain. You have to put some work into it. Tinker with the banister

notall2gether: You are right. I should be more proactive

Godotwait4me: Is your Dad mad that you two don't get along?

notall2gether: He was. Not anymore. He died a year ago

Godotwait4me: Sorry

Godotwait4me: What about your mom?

notall2gether: I killed her.

Godotwait4me: Did they take you to prison? Did you get to wear orange jumpsuit and fight for soap?

notall2gether: I think they fight for cigarettes

Godotwait4me: Whatever, it's still sexy.

notall2gether: Now I know what my next Halloween costume will be

Godotwait4me: Seriously though. Where's Mom?

notall2gether: No idea.

Godotwait4me: She left you?

notall2gether: Ouch.

Godotwait4me: Sorry.

notall2gether: It's cool. Mom was good with magic. Here today/gone the next.

Godotwait4me: I'd never go see her show if that's how she treats you.

In fact, I'd burn down her whole act.

notall2gether: Aw, arson for me??

Godotwait4me: Damn right :)

notall2gether: Why did your parents divorce?

Godotwait4me: Dad got tired of being cheated on

notall2gether: Oh

Godotwait4me: Some guys just can't handle a little adultery

notall2gether: How are you and your Mom?

Godotwait4me: She keeps doing things to piss me off

notall2gether: Like?

Godotwait4me: Breathing

notall2gether: Do I need to come over and tinker with your banister?

Godotwait4me: We don't have a staircase but you should come over anyway

notall2gether: Why

Godotwait4me: So I can see the face of my fav matchmaker

notall2gether: It's a normal face

Godotwait4me: Doubt it

notall2gether: Swear

Godotwait4me: Send pic

notall2gether: NO

Godotwait4me: Why

notall2gether: It's late. Ttyl

Godotwait4me: K. Did I say something wrong?

notall2gether: No

Godotwait4me: Is it bc I called you Rain? It was stupid. Won't tease you again.

notall2gether: I'll text tomorrow.

Godotwait4me: Really?

notall2gether: Really. Btw Rain is kind of pretty

I Am NOT

Excited that Godot texted me
I am NOT in my room doing mental cartwheels
I am NOT squealing excitedly into my pillow
I am NOT writing this moment down

The Next Day

Share news with BFFs
Boots chokes on her fry
Dash does actual cartwheel
Later while headed to class
I spot crush Blake Harrison
I don't feel guilty
About gawking
Just because I'm in
Heaven with Godot
     Does not mean—can't look down
     Every now and then . . .
Blake more than a pretty face
Kelly made comment
About me in class
With no class
     They laughed
     He didn't

Blake Harrison Is a Puzzle

Wonder how pretty I'd have to be
To get close enough
To solving him . . .

It's Been a Few Days

And Godot and I speak
ALL the time
I am sure that other things are going on
People working, women giving birth
Concerts being held and new apps to download
But I could not care less
Boots on the other hand
Does not share my tunnel vision
She is forever nagging me about meeting Godot
In the real world
(Yeah, like I'd ruin the best thing ever)

Firetrash.com is now
Popular all over town
With users from
Neighboring schools
But Dash thinks
Godot may be someone from
Our school
Our school?
Ha! No way anyone as
Amazing as
Godot
Could come from our school
Boots suggests
The real Godot is
A billionaire's son, a dashing young lord

A lonely rock star
But they don't need to make up anything
Godotwait4me is a guy who likes talking to me
That's more than enough

Aside From

My suddenly booming online social life there is the matter
    of the Halloween dance
It coats every conversation at school after school
And the dreams of everyone in White Noise
Boots is going with Dave Cuttler
I'm not sure she really likes him, but he has
William Shatner's autograph, and, well
That's all she needed to say yes

Dash Wants

To go with Sam
He's had a crush on him since last year
He tries to work up to it every day
And every day he finds a reason not to
Today's reason:
How can I even think about that right now
What with global warming?

Not Even Kara

Could dim my shine
Every time I get a text
From him I feel like
First rose to bloom
In spring
First sunny day after
Months of endless
Alaskan nights

My Sunny Disposition

Cannot blind me to what is happening
Boots is missing school more and more
Her headaches are coming more often
She tries to downplay it
Last week I caught her crying during
In-class movie
"Pain of migraine?" I asked
But she insisted movie got to her
But I don't know anyone
Who would weep during
Tom Sawyer

Dash Notices Too

But she won't allow us
To talk about it
We have yet to learn how to hide our fear
That she is getting worse
She doesn't want us to worry
Yet another thing we have not learned
How to do

The Three of Us Go Out

To shop for things
We don't need more of
Books. Magazines. Video games.
We enter a shady, smoky shop
Off Mont Street
They sell
What America needs more of
Cigarettes. Pipes. Porn.
As a joke I buy
A large picture book
Getting to Know the Female Body
For Dash
He squirms
We laugh
It is awesome

A Few Days Later
Dash's dad finds it
He thinks it is a sign of hope

You Have to Tell Him
Are the words we keep shoving at Dash
He is less than receptive

His dad is *finally* proud
How can he give that up?
How can we make him?

I Remind
Him to ask Sam to the dance
He says today is not the day
Reason #104:
It's bad luck to ask someone out on the third Wednesday of the
    month.
Dash reminds me
I have been avoiding something too
But there is no avoiding
I just won't ever meet Godot
He won't like me in person
Why bother?
In his head
I'm a thin, pretty starlet

Why ruin it for him or me?
"Sooner or later . . .
This guy will want to see you"
Boots warns

Yet They're Right
More and more, Godot
Pushes for us to meet
Please. Please.
Just a little while longer . . .

Godotwait4me: Rain?

notall2gether: Yeah

Godotwait4me: What's up?

notall2gether: My blood pressure

Godotwait4me: Why?

notall2gether: Step Satan on war path

Godotwait4me: Why

notall2gether: Wants me to go to therapy

Godotwait4me: Bc of your Dad?

notall2gether: No bc therapy is cool now

Godotwait4me: Sucks. But it may be easier to just go

notall2gether: I don't need it

Godotwait4me: Did you tell her that?

notall2gether: It's like when I talk she just hears duck sounds. She never listens

Godotwait4me: Not her fault. It's a condition that comes with age

notall2gether: Like wrinkles

Godotwait4me: Like lying

notall2gether: What's up with you?

Godotwait4me: Mom bought me and sis new ipads

notall2gether: Hating you rn

Godotwait4me: She only did it to make up for Dad leaving

notall2gether: She wants to buy your love. Aww . . .

Godotwait4me: She's just started paying for what she did

notall2gether: You gonna bleed her dry?

Godotwait4me: No access to firing squad so yes

notall2gether: Hey, can I put a few people in the line of fire too?

Godotwait4me: Step Satan?

notall2gether: And a girl at school. Kelly

Godotwait4me: Why

notall2gether: It's just the right thing to do

Godotwait4me: Let me guess, she is like 2% cuter than you. And you hate that

notall2gether: I'm not that shallow. She is 2.5% cuter and that is why she must die!

Godotwait4me: My mistake

notall2gether: How's the ipad?

Godotwait4me: Can't lie; it's awesome. Lot of apps and the resolution is amazing

notall2gether: Yeah, gonna have to send a little more hate your way

Godotwait4me: How about sending a pic my way? Why are you hiding?

notall2gether: Why are you? You never sent me a pic.

Godotwait4me: Ok, I send you one and you send me one, right?

notall2gether: Um . . . it's more fun this way. Guessing what the other looks like.

Godotwait4me: You don't want to leave it up to my imagination. I can be . . . R rated

notall2gether: I can be X rated at times

Godotwait4me: Flirt

notall2gether: What do you think I look like?

Godotwait4me: 10 eyeballs, 8 arms and 4 fingers

notall2gether: Close but I only have 7 eyeballs

Godotwait4me: Damn

notall2gether: You lose

Godotwait4me: Is there a consolation prize?

notall2gether: Washer/dryer and lifetime supply of Thai noodles in a can

Godotwait4me: Variety pack?

notall2gether: Of course

Godotwait4me: Then it was all worth it. I've been thinking about you all day

notall2gether: Good things?

Godotwait4me: Naughty things

notall2gether: Even better

Godotwait4me: I bet you have soft lips

notall2gether: I ordered the 7 arms/soft lip package so yes

Godotwait4me: I dreamed about kissing you last night

notall2gether: And . . .

Godotwait4me: It was spectacular

notall2gether: You didn't get farther than that did you?

Godotwait4me: No. I was respectful

notall2gether: Liar

Godotwait4me: I'd love to do it in person

notall2gether: Do it?

Godotwait4me: I mean kiss, not sex. Not that I wouldn't want to . . . I just mean . . . would bashing my

Godotwait4me: Head on the wall make better words come out my mouth?

notall2gether: No but it's cool. I get it

Godotwait4me: Do you?

notall2gether: Yeah, you want to kiss a girl you never met bc you like the words she puts on the screen before you

Godotwait4me: No. I want to kiss the girl who's been killing me with her humor and stories. The girl who makes me feel . . . not so out there

notall2gether: What if she doesn't live up to what you think? What if she is . . . not pretty

Godotwait4me: Doubt it

notall2gether: I gotta go

Godotwait4me: Why do you do that?

notall2gether: What?

Godotwait4me: Run

notall2gether: Maybe I want you to chase me

Godotwait4me: Do you?

notall2gether: Sometimes

Godotwait4me: Am I supposed to woo you?

notall2gether: Woo? Maybe you are old

Godotwait4me: No, just corny

notall2gether: Yes, woo me.

Godotwait4me: Okay, but don't be surprised if you fall for me

notall2gether: Why would I do that?

Godotwait4me: Common courtesy: fall for guy who woos you

notall2gether: Haha

Godotwait4me: Not joking

notall2gether: Really?

Godotwait4me: Really.

Everything in My World Has Been

Paused.

Nothing moves except my heart

It leaps out of my room into the sky

Hangs just above the earth's orbit

It is not alone

He is out there too

He is out there too . . .

It's Official

Blake Harrison and I are over
(We were together in my head)
But I don't need a pretend guy
Have real
Guy
Well
"Real"
Guy
Godot.
My guy.

Looking at Blake Harrison
Standing in the middle of
A group of friends laughing loud
Putting on a brave, strong face
Knowing all the while his
Imaginary girl
Has left him
Poor guy—he's heartbroken . . .

Meanwhile Kelly Canyon

Keeps making pig sounds anytime I'm near
Her other friends snicker and laugh when I walk past
I did the wrong assignment
Left lunch money at home
Failed. Pop. Quiz. In two classes.
Boots gave me a hug to make up for the day I was having

Dash's Days

Are going fairly well too
His dad has been acting like a dad
They watch movies, play games, and crack jokes.
Dash high with pride
Shows off Dad like giddy girl with rock engagement ring
When he tells his dad the truth
Rock will be appraised and found to have
No real value

It's a Drug

Dash explains that Dad's acceptance is a true high
Boots and I look down below
We worry about the fall
Yet we can't deny
The change in him
It's in the spring of his step. The certainty in his stride.
Dash Montgomery is
Loved
By the one person who never gave it to him before and he
    feels
G   O   O   D

Boots Flinches
Slightly
Her head hurts again

Before I launch
Into how stubborn she is and how she refuses to admit
    she's unwell
I guess I should let her speak for herself
But whatever she says, I did have an alibi
For here is my favorite Trekkie

Lisa Thomas (AKA Boots)

Payment
When I was four I wanted a new bike for my birthday
I was told to pray
God would give it to me
For weeks I was faithfully praying
Birthday came and went
No bike
I tried Santa. Left him a plate of Double Stuff Oreos
Xmas morning got new bike
Guess God needed an offering
After news of illness, Mom went to church and prayed
I went online
Googled *What to get the guy who has everything*

The Clocks

I made my parents get rid of all the clocks in the house

Now Dad is always late for work

Mom is always early

Didn't tell them about the small stopwatch under my pillow

Or the tick and the tock between the silence of everyday living

Live Long and Prosper

I became a Trekkie after I was diagnosed

No one in outer space ever gets tumors

But We Laugh Too

Parents had to give up lots of things

Sleep, stillness, sanity

All for my condition

We replaced it with

Board games. Road trips. Campfires.

That means we spend hours in the car headed to campsite

Arguing over last night's Scrabble game

And *woot* is not a word!

BOOTS

My body turned against me

Waged war

Now I am dressed and suited accordingly

Mr. North

And I don't get along

His homework is too hard

Takes too long to figure out

He gives homework no matter what

When I was in hospital people sent

Cards. Flowers. Prayers.

Mr. North sent

Homework

He is now my favorite teacher

Solid Foundation

Dash and I have nothing in common

Except our love of

B   O   Y   S

And, well, that's . . .

Everything

Punishment

I don't wash dishes when my mom tells me to
I never turn in homework on the day that it is due
I leave the TV on when I go to bed
Mean to turn lights off; leave them on instead
I've let a few secrets out. Maybe two or three.
Can that be the reason this has happened to me?

Forever

Actually I like being bald
Enter a room everyone turns
They'll always remember me

My Shay

Gonna get that girl to try turkey bacon
Someday
Someday . . .

There

I couldn't look

What did she say about me?

Just tell me this

Were the words *turkey* and *bacon* used?

I knew it!

Luckily

None of that matters

'Cause flashing light on cell indicates text awaits

Teacher talks

Forever. Clock laughs.

S l o w s d o w n . . . then . . . stops.

C'mon!

Flashing light on cell indicates: he thinks of me.

Checked cell—battery dead.

C'mon!

Flashing light indicates: he needs me

Run home. Rain begins. Cat jumps, startled.

I fall flat on face

C'mon!

Flashing light indicates: he wants me.

Home. Finally. In front of screen.

I am not alone.

> **Godotwait4me:** Is it sad being around your friend all the time knowing that she's . . . ?

notall2gether: At first but now we just have fun and don't think about it

Godotwait4me: I would think about it all the time

notall2gether: I think about it mostly when we say goodbye. Sometimes I will hug her so tight, she says she's being "loved to death." She says it's torture. She has filed several complaints with Amnesty International.

Godotwait4me: And you still do it? You are a cruel girl

notall2gether: If I knew I was seeing my Dad for the last time the day before he died I would have held on to him tighter. And for much longer. I would have done things different ya know?

Godotwait4me: Like what?

notall2gether: Like not said I hate you

Godotwait4me: That's the last thing you said to him?

notall2gether: He was planning another get to love your stepmom weekend and I freaked. Great daughter huh?

Godotwait4me: You were just venting. He knows you loved him

notall2gether: For the past year all we did was fight.

Godotwait4me: I didn't talk to my Mom for weeks after Dad left

notall2gether: And now?

Godotwait4me: Oh we have in-depth convos (When's dinner? What's for dinner? Why did you make that for dinner?)

notall2gether: Deep Oprah-type stuff, I see

Godotwait4me: There's no need to say more ya know? She can see the truth in my face

notall2gether: Which is?

Godotwait4me: That it's all her fault. She messed up our fam just to get boned

notall2gether: Maybe she couldn't help it

Godotwait4me: Adults are supposed to have control

notall2gether: Then I say it's a myth. Like Bigfoot, Loch Ness Monster, and decent fat-free ice cream . . .

Godotwait4me: Too bad. I liked thinking when I get old, everything would be all right

notall2gether: Maybe your dad will come back

Godotwait4me: He can't look her in the eye. He's gone forever.

notall2gether: You want to be with him and not her?

Godotwait4me: Yeah but he doesn't want me

notall2gether: How do you know?

Godotwait4me: I asked to go live with him and he said no

notall2gether: Why?

Godotwait4me: Said he can't cook and clean. He can't afford a housekeeper blah, blah, bull @!$@$%. He just didn't want me

notall2gether: He thinks your mom would be better at taking care of things

Godotwait4me: She doesn't take care of things; she destroy things. I will never forgive her

notall2gether: Maybe if you learn to cook, your Dad would take you in. lol

Godotwait4me: Who says I can't cook?

notall2gether: What? You suck. How could you hold out on me like that. What can you cook?

Godotwait4me: K, I can't cook. But I microwave real good. I mean top of the line

notall2gether: I'm impressed

Godotwait4me: Are you?

notall2gether: Very

Godotwait4me: With the micro thing or with me?

notall2gether: Both

Godotwait4me: Rain?

notall2gether: Yeah?

Godotwait4me: Why doesn't he want me?

notall2gether: idk

Godotwait4me: . . .

> **notall2gether:** I want you. Does that make it a little better?

> **Godotwait4me:** No

> **notall2gether:** Oh

> **Godotwait4me:** It makes it a lot better . . .

I'm Sure

I woke up, dressed, ate
Attended some type of class where lessons were taught
But I can't remember any of it

My Life

A series of delicious texts and sinfully decadent exchanges

> **Godotwait4me:** Rain?

> **notall2gether:** Hey, I thought you were gonna be camping all weekend

> **Godotwait4me:** I was, but my friend got grounded. His rents called off the trip

notall2gether: Sucks. Why?

Godotwait4me: They caught him doing it

notall2gether: With who?

Godotwait4me: Himself

notall2gether: He was . . .

Godotwait4me: Yeah

notall2gether: By himself?

Godotwait4me: Um . . . yeah

notall2gether: Wow, I know his fam freaked but why is he grounded?

Godotwait4me: Catholics

notall2gether: Oh

Godotwait4me: They are making him go back to bible class

notall2gether: Guess the first time didn't take

Godotwait4me: He thought he locked the door . . . His mom came in . . . now she won't get out of bed

Godotwait4me: She thinks she raised him wrong

notall2gether: Is it that serious?

Godotwait4me: They are devout

notall2gether: Guess it's good I don't believe in anything huh?

Godotwait4me: Why, you please yourself a lot?

notall2gether: Maybe

Godotwait4me: Too late for shyness. How often do you do it?

notall2gether: You can't ask me that

Godotwait4me: Why

116

notall2gether: Bc I'm a girl

Godotwait4me: Girls do it, that I know. I just want to know how often

notall2gether: Like 2x a month

Godotwait4me: That's hot

notall2gether: You?

Godotwait4me: Never. I only allow pure thoughts into my head.

Godotwait4me: I am not sure we should remain friends as you may corrupt me

notall2gether: C'mon

Godotwait4me: Seriously. Last week I got the new Jay Z joint. Now this.

Godotwait4me: I'm being corrupted from inside out. I can feel it. How is a boy

Godotwait4me: supposed to protect his innocence?

notall2gether: Fine don't tell me

Godotwait4me: Ok, ok, I do it 2x

notall2gether: A month?

Godotwait4me: A day

notall2gether: WTF?

Godotwait4me: It's on my "to-do list" so
. . . I do it!

notall2gether: What do you think about?

Godotwait4me: Snow cones, opera and
springtime

notall2gether: Seriously

Godotwait4me: T&A, sex scenes and
certain people

notall2gether: Like who?

Godotwait4me: Beyoncé

notall2gether: After buying her husband's music? Traitor. Anyone else?

Godotwait4me: Scarlett Johansson

notall2gether: Oh. She's nice . . . anyone else?

Godotwait4me: Besides you, no

notall2gether: Really!!!

Godotwait4me: All the time

notall2gether: But you don't know what I look like

Godotwait4me: I kind of have your voice in my head. When I'm doing it

Godotwait4me: I hear you tell me things. And it's sexy as $@$#$

notall2gether: What kind of things?

Godotwait4me: How much you like it. How much you like me. And how good it feels

notall2gether: I'm glad to know I'm so complimentary in your head

Godotwait4me: And giving

notall2gether: I bet

Godotwait4me: So . . . what do you think about (and don't get shy on me). It's your turn

notall2gether: I think about doing Jay Z to cheer him up since his wife has left him all alone to be with you

Godotwait4me: C'mon Rain. What do you think about?

notall2gether: Hands. Kissing. Hair stroking

Godotwait4me: Awwww

notall2gether: Whatever :)

Godotwait4me: Do you ever cast anyone in a role?

notall2gether: Yeah, I casted you

Godotwait4me: Really???

notall2gether: Yeah, you're the bellhop Jay Z and I ring for when hours of acrobatic sex leave us dehydrated

Godotwait4me: Do I get to watch?

notall2gether: Sure why not

Godotwait4me: For real, Rain. Do you think about me when you are alone, doing it?

notall2gether: I haven't been doing it bc lately I have had something better

Godotwait4me: What?

notall2gether: This

Godotwait4me: Night?

notall2gether: Night

He Lingers

In the milk in my cereal
The sound in my steps. The music in my laughter.
He fills spaces between my pauses

In My Mind's Eye

We've been traveling
Godot and I cross oceans, hop islands, space walk
We've had lunch at the Louvre
Dinner at the Plaza, breakfast in bed
He's painted, serenaded, and
Loved me

It's Early

Too early for him to be online
So I send a poem in hopes that
Just contacting him will hold me over

How You'll Know (That I Like You)

I am usually a Times New Roman girl
Every now and then I get wild
And I throw in some
Arial Black
Then there was the time I got reckless
Gave in to peer pressure and used
MATISSE ITC
But today just for you I will bend
I will shape, I will sculpt
Everything I am
And give you
Edwardian Script
(Wow, when did I become such a flirt?)

Is Anything

Supposed to feel this good?
Won't the gods come tear us apart?
We've stolen all the world's happiness and
Poured it all into texts

Maybe the Gods

Don't yet know what we have taken from them
When they do, how swift will their justice be?
How much will this cost us?

Godotwait4me: So . . . you have 2 bffs. 1 is gay and the other is sick. A lot to deal with

notall2gether: They are the ones who have to put up with me mostly

Godotwait4me: You seem super easy to get along with

notall2gether: I'm a hard one but I've got my reasons . . .

Godotwait4me: Is that from Desperado?

notall2gether: OMG, you know it?

Godotwait4me: My Dad loves those old people songs.

notall2gether: My Dad too! He used to play them all the time

Godotwait4me: What exactly does it mean to "ride fences"?

notall2gether: idk. Maybe it's like something they used to do in the 60s like burning bras

Godotwait4me: I can't believe you know that song

notall2gether: Sad but true. I was the only 6 yr old to know all the words to American Pie.

Godotwait4me: Long version?

notall2gether: Yeah, Dad said the short version was crap

Godotwait4me: I got my Dad a double CD of oldies for fathers day last year. I wish I didn't

notall2gether: Why

Godotwait4me: I think it makes him . . . sad

notall2gether: But he still liked it. It's a good kind of sad

Godotwait4me: ???

notall2gether: I mean he's gonna be sad anyway so it might as well be to his fav tune, right?

Godotwait4me: I guess . . . Hey?

notall2gether: What?

Godotwait4me: Dance with me?

notall2gether: Via text?

Godotwait4me: Yeah. Wherever you are. Stop and be with me

notall2gether: K, what are we dancing to?

Godotwait4me: I have the perfect song. My parents danced to it at their wedding. It's their song. I'm sending you a youtube link

notall2gether: "Have I told you lately"?

Godotwait4me: Rod Stewart, is that cool?

notall2gether: Lol. Not by any stretch of the imagination. Let's do it!

[Please wait for music to load]

notall2gether: That was sweet, but everyone at Starbucks thinks I'm crazy now bc of you

notall2gether: I'm going to have to relocate. Thx Godot!

Godotwait4me: I'm sure you look great. Didn't know you could dance

notall2gether: I'm the best dancer at St. Bernadette's

Godotwait4me: Is that your school?

notall2gether: No. It's from Grease! Dash said any self-respecting gay boy

notall2gether: has to have a bff with extensive musical theater knowledge

Godotwait4me: Well he is doing a good job with you

notall2gether: Thanks, I actually really like the song you picked. And the part where he says

notall2gether: "ease my troubles, that's what you do" that reminds me of us

Godotwait4me: Me too

notall2gether: It's late. Gotta go. Dance again soon?

Godotwait4me: It's a date

notall2gether: Night

Godotwait4me: Night

Love.

Fake like I know how it works
Everyone else does

Later We Ask Boots About Her Health

She dodges the question with skilled, rehearsed moves
Dash pushes for more info; she declines
We sit in silence, our sorrow-coated eyes dry like deserts

128

She hates when we cry, so we keep it in
(Mostly)

Maybe She's Just Getting the Flu
I throw out in desperation
Dash leaps at it and holds on for dear life

And the Headaches?
Well, Dash and I agree it's from stress, homework, and junk
She is just fine . . .

notall2gether: Boots wants to have sex

Godotwait4me: Cool. Can I watch?

notall2gether: Be serious. She should wait

Godotwait4me: Isn't she ya know . . .

notall2gether: Yeah, she's dying but not today. She should wait until . . .

Godotwait4me: There is no until for her. She has to live in the moment. It's all she has

notall2gether: So bc she is short on time, she can do what she wants?

Godotwait4me: Let's say it's your last days. What are you doing?

notall2gether: You

Godotwait4me: Seriously?

notall2gether: It's my last days on earth right?

Godotwait4me: Yeah

notall2gether: So . . . yeah

Godotwait4me: That's the only way you would have sex with me?

notall2gether: No, if you had a deadly illness, I'd do you

Godotwait4me: Awww

notall2gether: But I would not be good at it

Godotwait4me: Yes you would

notall2gether: No, I am not sure where everything goes

Godotwait4me: Will send you instruction manual

notall2gether: So . . . you have done it before?

Godotwait4me: Kind of

notall2gether: ???

Godotwait4me: I got close then my stupid sis came home and we had to stop

notall2gether: Oh. So you got a girl?

Godotwait4me: It was last year

notall2gether: So she is not your girl now?

Godotwait4me: No

notall2gether: Why

Godotwait4me: She liked some other guy

notall2gether: Sucks. How far did you two get?

Godotwait4me: I took off her underwear

notall2gether: And . . .

Godotwait4me: Sis came home

notall2gether: Did she see you?

Godotwait4me: No. I am world's fastest dresser. Nearly had heart attack

notall2gether: Shame to be so young and get so close to death

Godotwait4me: All that and I didn't even get to do it

notall2gether: Did you not try again?

Godotwait4me: She went to spend the summer with her aunt. Met new guy

notall2gether: You miss her?

Godotwait4me: not since it has begun to "Rain"

notall2gether: Are you always this sweet?

Godotwait4me: Yes, aren't I adorable?

notall2gether: And humble

Godotwait4me: Glad you noticed

notall2gether: I haven't had sex yet

Godotwait4me: How far have you gotten?

notall2gether: Farther than my dad would have wanted. Not as far as I would have liked

133

Godotwait4me: Details

notall2gether: He took off my bra and touched me a little

Godotwait4me: Lucky guy

Godotwait4me: Then what?

notall2gether: Nothing

Godotwait4me: Why

notall2gether: I chickened out

Godotwait4me: Why

notall2gether: He was in the math club

Godotwait4me: And your body rejects future mathematicians?

notall2gether: The whole time he would rather have been doing fractions

Godotwait4me: What happened after?

notall2gether: We ordered a pizza and he helped me with my algebra

Godotwait4me: Nice guy

notall2gether: We were just friends

Godotwait4me: Is that what we are?

notall2gether: Is that all you want us to be?

Godotwait4me: idk

Godotwait4me: Let's meet. I want to hang with you in real world

notall2gether: Been to real world; not much there

Godotwait4me: There's you. I don't even know what your laugh sounds like

notall2gether: It's not all that impressive

Godotwait4me: Bugs Bunny like?

notall2gether: More Daffy Duck

Godotwait4me: Ohhh my fav.

notall2gether: It's late. Gotta go :)

Lately

Dash has done away with bright-colored tees
Advertising love for sale
He now wears monotone everything that allows him to
Blend

The Difference Between Him

And the White Noise is the difference between
White and off-white
In short my friend is

Fading

When Asked About

Change, Dash insists he's simply experimenting
He's trying out straight boys' skin

Even His Walk Has Changed

He used to glide down the hallway
Mark each step with his vibrant, sparkling bounce
Now he walks down the hallway
Marks each step with the sound of uniform
Sameness

We Watch As

Dash breaks apart from the inside
He's been great in my eyes
Never shrinking in the face of
Soul-sucking succubi
Who aim to leave merely a shell
He has never failed to
Rail. Rally. Rage.
Against the many
till now

His Undoing

Is for his dad
Figures if he breaks himself up
Gathers himself back together
He'll be a different person

Bring Up the Subject

Of Sam and the dance again
Dash shrugs and gives us
Reason #185:
Ask someone out during a full moon???

Dance Overdrive (A Nursery Rhyme)

Sally from English thought John would ask
But two weeks have since passed
She put her hopes on Peter
Maybe he would need her
Peter came through and asked her to go
But only if Kay says no
Carl wants to go with Jill
Who's not too cute but still . . .
Jill has eyes for Jack
But already said yes, can't take it back
Matt wants to go with Terry but she's too tall
Who wants to tiptoe kiss after all?
Mandy is going with Mark
'Cause he can stay out past dark
Every girl's found someone to take her
Be it the butcher or the baker
Me, I'll be home doing just fine
Got everything I need online.

Then Again

I can picture it now
Entering the gym, Godot by my side
The elegance of our entrance makes each pair of eyes stay
    on us
While we dance, laugh, and cuddle, people look on,
    bewildered
That gorgeous, sexy, charming girl, she looks like Shay
    Summers
But, how, *how* can that be . . . ?

One Thing I Hate

About seeing Godot only online?
The dances we won't dance
The movies we won't see
The hands we won't hold

Then Meet Him in the Real World

Think to myself
What Godot and I have now is amazing
Could we survive IRL?
Never.

notall2gether: G, what's up?

Godotwait4me: If my house burned down with me in it, it would fall right in line with the day I been having

notall2gether: That bad?

Godotwait4me: Can't begin to tell you

notall2gether: Try

Godotwait4me: Why? You gonna fix it?

notall2gether: Yeah, I know people

Godotwait4me: Thx but I don't think you can help me

notall2gether: What happened?

Godotwait4me: Rents fighting for property. Who owned what and when

notall2gether: Sorry

Godotwait4me: Why would they get married if they were just gonna split?

Godotwait4me: What was the point?

notall2gether: I don't think they knew

Godotwait4me: She knew. She knew she would never be faithful. So why say yes to a guy

Godotwait4me: if you're gonna break his heart a few years later?

notall2gether: I guess things don't turn out the way you think they will

Godotwait4me: Yeah like you and me

notall2gether: ???

Godotwait4me: I thought if I found a really cool chick who was silly, smart and sweet, she and

Godotwait4me: I would hang all the time. But you want nothing to do with me

notall2gether: That's not true. You know how I feel about you

Godotwait4me: Yeah, you like me so much you never want to see me

notall2gether: Don't be like that

Godotwait4me: Yeah. I know. I gotta be the "understanding" type.

Godotwait4me: The guy who lets you take your time and go the pace you want.

Godotwait4me: But I have spent the last 2 hours listening to my dad fight to keep

Godotwait4me: a summer house harder than he fought to keep me

notall2gether: I'm sorry about that

Godotwait4me: I don't feel like being understanding. I feel like seeing you, let's meet up in 30.

notall2gether: I can't

Godotwait4me: Why

notall2gether: Bc I'm not ready

Godotwait4me: When will you be?

notall2gether: idk

Godotwait4me: Thx Rain, that's really helpful

[Godotwait4me has logged off]

All the While My Friends Still Tried to Find

Reasons why I should meet up with Godot

He could be foreign = *Shay, it's your duty as an American*

He could be from another galaxy = *Shay, it's your duty as an earthling*

He could be hot = *Shay, it's your duty as a gay boy's best friend*

They Found Reasons

Hiding in places I never thought to look
Beneath mattress. Behind fridge. Back of closet.
I kindly rejected each with courteous letter

Dear Reason & Logic, Inc.:
Shay Summers no longer
1. Needs
2. Desires
       Nor
3. Requires your services.
She will seek representation from competitor
Irrational Joy & Blind Bliss, Inc.
Ms. Summers thanks you for your years of service

Boots Would Like

Me to invest in the self-help section of the bookstore
She points out that low self-esteem can hold people back in life
Dash points out that big girls like me are sexy
I point out the hour
We are late for class

Judging from Our Texts

Godot's really into us meeting
But why
Why risk A Good Thing?

144

Speaking of Good Things

Dash is bursting with excitement
His dad's company is having its annual father-and-son golf
    tournament
For the first time his dad invited him

At What Point

Should we remind him
He can't golf?
Should we do it before
Or after he remembers
How long it took him
To make contact with the ball
When we played miniature golf?
Oh, and when exactly should you point out the hideous
Plaid, throw-up-colored golf pants?

Before He Tells You

He has his heart set on it
Damn it!

Dash's Dad

Sat him on the bed, put arms around him
Told him how proud he'd be
To have his son by his side
Win or lose

Parents

Should be made to take many classes
Before kids can be had
First period:
How not to make your kid feel like #%#$
Second period:
Gay sons and daughters
Third period:
Stepmom and why your kid will never like her

Sweetie, You Have to Tell Him

Boots and I find honeyed words to coat the cold reality pill
Dash has to swallow

Dash Speaks Softly

Years guessing
How to win his love
Finally
I found a way

All I have to do is
Be someone else

Dash Insists

Maybe I'm not even gay
Could have been a phase
A moment in time
And time
Passes . . .

Boots Cries Out

We rush over.
Her breath
Labored. Slow. Shallow.
We start to call for help
She won't let us
Puts on brave face so often
We hardly remember what she really looks like

We Take Her

Home
Where she makes us swear not to tell her
Mom

Chocolate Would Rescue Me

From feeling so defeated

But I'm hoping Godot gets there first

notall2gether: G, you still mad at me?

Godotwait4me: I'm not mad. I just don't get it

notall2gether: We are having such a good time here, why go out there?

Godotwait4me: So I can touch you and know that my girl is real. Not some letters on a screen

notall2gether: I am real

Godotwait4me: How would I know that?

notall2gether: I just need some time

Godotwait4me: Is there another guy?

notall2gether: No

Godotwait4me: A girl?

notall2gether: No

Godotwait4me: You old?

notall2gether: No. please stop

Godotwait4me: Then tell me why you don't want to see me?

notall2gether: I do.

Godotwait4me: So . . .

notall2gether: So I have had a #%$^#$ day. Dash is lying to his dad and he's gonna get hurt in the end.

notall2gether: Boots isn't doing well and she won't admit it

Godotwait4me: I'm sorry about your friend. What can I do?

149

notall2gether: idk

Godotwait4me: If Dash is gay, he has to get to a point where he can tell his dad on his own.

Godotwait4me: You can't push him. And Boots

Godotwait4me: is the same thing. She has to face that she's not well

notall2gether: I just want them to be okay. They are all I have

Godotwait4me: That's not true. You have me

notall2gether: Thx. It means a lot

Godotwait4me: I wish I could hold you. Make it better

notall2gether: I wish that too

Godotwait4me: This is crazy! Why wish? Let's just meet up.

notall2gether: Let's talk about something else

Godotwait4me: See that's the thing. There is nothing else. You are all

Godotwait4me: I think about. Getting a text from you makes everything ok

notall2gether: It does the same for me

Godotwait4me: But how many times can we act like it's enough?

notall2gether: Why isn't it enough?

Godotwait4me: Bc it isn't

notall2gether: Let's not do this. Talk about something else, please

Godotwait4me: Why do you have to control everything?

notall2gether: I don't

Godotwait4me: It's like you are too scared

Godotwait4me: to let go

notall2gether: What if we meet and you hate me?

Godotwait4me: Why would I do that?

notall2gether: I don't look like . . .

Godotwait4me: You don't look like what?

notall2gether: Never mind.

Godotwait4me: Help me Rain, please help me understand

notall2gether: This thing . . . you and me . . . it's so good. I don't want to mess it up

Godotwait4me: Meeting can only make it better. Please do this for me notall2gether: I want to but . . .

Godotwait4me: But you don't want it enough. K. No prob

notall2gether: Godot? . . . Hello?

[Godotwait4me has logged off]

One Day I Saw

A clown on a bus
A nun on a bike
A stripper at the Laundromat
I don't know what forces allowed
All these people to be there at the same time
But there they were
That day was very much like today

Where Do I Start?

Kara signed me up for yoga!
　　　　How much would it cost to hire an assassin?
Seriously. I have two hundred dollars saved up.
Where does one go to buy one?
Is there a union?
　　　　A payment plan?
Can I get a school discount?

Does it cost extra if they make it messy and
painful?
Is there a website?
A blog?

Dash Is Taking Golf Lessons!

And missing like THREE *Project Runway* episodes
BACK TO BACK!
Oh, how dark the days!
And Boots
Well, she is almost nowhere to be found
Too busy trying to dodge us
She is so crafty
She hides behind basketball team members
Navigates through crowds like DiCaprio
Catch Me If You Can

And Then There's Godot

We haven't traveled in my head in days
I don't mean to upset him
I'm just trying to hold on to the best thing
That's happened to me

How Much

Can I fight this?
He's like sand through my fingers
It's only for the moment . . .

When I Get Home

Kara informs me
She was well-meaning
In the yoga thing
I inform her
I have long since
Tuned her out

I Try to Stay Away

Give Godot some space
But I miss him more than I thought I could
Texts should come with warnings:
*CAUTION: You may get addicted to the guy you chat with and
    then have to give it all up cold turkey*

Keeping Busy

Is my rehab
Clean room. Empty trash. Do homework.
Don't look at screen
He's not there

Do homework. Have dinner. Read book.
Don't wait for text
It's not coming
Do crossword. Text friends. Surf web.
Don't email
There'll be no reply

Screw It!

My will has failed me

notall2gether: Godot, you there?

Godotwait4me: Yes

notall2gether: So . . . how are you?

Godotwait4me: Fine

notall2gether: Me too

Godotwait4me: K

notall2gether: How's things at home?

Godotwait4me: It's whatever

notall2gether: Yeah, I know what you mean. I heard Rod Stewart today.

notall2gether: Some lady was blasting it in her car and singing along like crazy

Godotwait4me: K

notall2gether: Godot

Godotwait4me: Yes

notall2gether: Let's dance

Godotwait4me: Can't. Homework

notall2gether: Maybe later?

Godotwait4me: Gotta go

notall2gether: Wait!

Godotwait4me: Yeah?

notall2gether: Good night . . .

I Walk Around the House
Like the world has ended
Because it has

If Dad Were Here
He'd tell me I was overreacting
I'd argue
Tell him Godot means the world to me
He'd smile and say
Give it a week

So I Do
I leave my room
And join the world

And All the World
Is getting ready for the dance
Girls fill the shops
Guys huddle in corners to review
Who has dates with whom

And Blake Harrison

Sits alone in the stairwell
What do you do when you catch Zeus alone?
Just a god and his thoughts

His Eyes

Sparks of green and gold
His hair dark like the ocean at night
Gracefully cascading down his face
Radiance of his smile
Lethal, impossible to escape
I should say hello
Mention that before Godot
I loved him
Planned two-kids-and-dog scenario
        But I don't
           In case Zeus scares easily

I Guess This Is Progress

Thinking of a different guy
There's no chance with Zeus
Still
Better to gaze at gods
Than blank screens

Godotwait4me: Rain, I wrote you a poem. I'm not good at that kind of stuff

Godotwait4me: But I thought you would like it or hate it. Idk

notall2gether: Wow, yeah, I'd love to read it

Godotwait4me: K, here goes. Don't laugh

notall2gether: Promise

[You have (1) unread message]

The moment
When he sees her
Pieces assemble
That he didn't know were missing

He fears living in a world
she's not in
He seeks to reassure
Her

She is queen of all
in his world

and if
this world
casts her out

she would
still
have
his
world
to call
home

When he sees her
Pieces assemble
That he didn't know were missing

Godotwait4me: It sucks right?

notall2gether: No, G. It's . . . thank you

Godotwait4me: You really like it?

notall2gether: So much . . .

Godotwait4me: I just wanted you to know that it's cool if you're . . . different or whatever.

notall2gether: Me too. All I want is to be with you

notall2gether: So . . . how about we talk on the phone?

Godotwait4me: It's already hard not to think about you. Hearing your voice would just make it

Godotwait4me: worse if you don't plan on seeing me. So, yeah we can talk on the phone

Godotwait4me: but only if you promise we will meet up sometime after

notall2gether: I can't promise that. I'm sorry

Godotwait4me: No, you're not. You don't care what this is doing to me

notall2gether: I do. I care about you so much

Dash's Love Life

Isn't going much better
The dance is only a few weeks away
The only thing he's worked on is his swing, his excuses,
And his straight-guy walk
Reason #314:
I can't ask Sam to the dance because my ancestors are from
That town in the movie Footloose *where dance is forbidden*
I have to honor their memory

The Word *Pig*

Is spray-painted on my locker
I didn't see her do it but I'm sure it was
Kelly Canyon
I'm not upset; I'm rather impressed
Didn't think she could spell
Yay public education!

Dash and Boots Offer to Retaliate

Mastermind
Intricate plot involving
Ecstasy. Whip cream. Mexican police.

There Is No Need for Revenge

I have plans to jump inside a
Triple-thick chocolate-
Chocolate-
Chip milkshake

My Brain Freezes Over

Due to the speed I'm inhaling
The chocolate-chip winter

Okay, I Will Agree to Meet Him

For once I will leap!
Leap!
Into the dream that good things happen
Even to girls like
Me

I Hear Pigs

Coming out of my backpack
Take a look
My cell makes pig sounds
Kelly Canyon laughs
She got hold of my cell

Changed: my ringtone
I change: my mind
No one is meeting anyone

Godotwait4me: Rain, I smoked for the first time last night

notall2gether: What?

Godotwait4me: Friends got some weed. Went to park near my house

notall2gether: How was it?

Godotwait4me: Tastes like burnt wood

notall2gether: Feels like?

Godotwait4me: Nothing mattered

notall2gether: Is that good?

Godotwait4me: Kind of

notall2gether: So, you gonna do it again?

Godotwait4me: Maybe

notall2gether: Are you planning on becoming a weed head?

Godotwait4me: I'm gonna pee first then become a weed head

notall2gether: Seriously. I think one time is enough

Godotwait4me: Why, Mom?

notall2gether: It's stupid

Godotwait4me: I'm stupid?

notall2gether: No but smoking is . . . lame

Godotwait4me: You never tried it and you are knocking it. No fair

166

notall2gether: I don't have to try drinking bleach to know I won't like it

notall2gether: It felt good?

Godotwait4me: Not at first. I coughed and stuff but after a few puffs, I was like floating

notall2gether: So you gonna get high all the time now?

Godotwait4me: Not if you are here to stop me. So . . . come over

notall2gether: The only way you will behave is if you get to see me?

Godotwait4me: Yes

notall2gether: Why

Godotwait4me: Bc I freaking like you. Why is that so hard for you to understand? I like you. Deal

notall2gether: Why are you so weird today. You high now?

Godotwait4me: Yeah, so what?

notall2gether: Text me when you are back to normal

Godotwait4me: You ok waiting 10 or 20 years

notall2gether: Godot . . .

Godotwait4me: That's not my damn name. Why don't you ask me my real name?

notall2gether: I like just the people we are online. It's fun

Godotwait4me: It's pathetic. We can't live here forever.

notall2gether: You want to stop talking?

Godotwait4me: I want to see you

notall2gether: No

Godotwait4me: Screw you then

notall2gether: What?

Godotwait4me: S-C-R-E-W you

notall2gether: What's wrong with you?

Godotwait4me: You girls are full of *%&$#. Just like my mom. She told Dad she was gonna be faithful then

Godotwait4me: he finds her at a skanky motel with another guy. All of you suck

notall2gether: Bye Godot

Godotwait4me: THAT IS NOT MY NAME!!!!

notall2gether: Whatever

Godotwait4me: You are a lying tease

I Am
Weaker
Than I'd like
Softer
Than I let on
Smaller
Than I'll admit
But I will
NOT
Be disrespected

I'm Not Agonizing
Over him
No really
I am pissed off and don't care
If he never texts again

Sometimes
You can't cry anymore
Ache anymore
Try anymore

Shay Summers
Shut down for the day

Godotwait4me: Thought I would say hi . . . Rain? . . . Rain?

Godotwait4me: Say something . . . K . . . good night . . .

Godotwait4me: Hello again . . . Look I know you're mad at me.

Godotwait4me: You can yell at me and curse me out but

Godotwait4me: First you have to text me back . . . . Hello? . . . Rain? . . .

Godotwait4me: I know you are not talking to me. I just wanted to say

Godotwait4me: I'm sorry . . . I miss you

notall2gether: G, stop texting. I'm no longer talking to you.

Godotwait4me: What can I do to make it up to you?

notall2gether: Nothing

Days Go By

The blacks and grays of his absence
Make it hard to be happy
I Miss Him

notall2gether: Hey, Smokey . . .

Godotwait4me: Rain?

notall2gether: Yeah

Godotwait4me: Hi :)

notall2gether: Hello

Godotwait4me: Didn't think I would hear from you again

notall2gether: You were such a jerk to me. And for no reason

Godotwait4me: I had just seen my mom and she told us about the actual day Dad caught her and I freaked.

Godotwait4me: Sorry

notall2gether: You were also high

Godotwait4me: Yeah

notall2gether: Is that an everyday thing now?

Godotwait4me: No, it was something I needed to try

notall2gether: You called me a lying tease and I didn't do anything to you.

Godotwait4me: I'm sorry

notall2gether: You think every girl is like your mom?

Godotwait4me: No, not every girl . . .

notall2gether: Next time you call me that, I'm gone. Got it?

Godotwait4me: Yeah

notall2gether: How's your dad?

Godotwait4me: He cries a lot

notall2gether: I didn't think guys do that

Godotwait4me: Same here. How's Step Satan?

notall2gether: She made me see a therapist

Godotwait4me: Wow, sucks

notall2gether: Her name is Dr. Dementia.

Godotwait4me: Seriously?

notall2gether: Yeah, it's pronounced differently but still . . .

Godotwait4me: When will we meet?

notall2gether: Not yet. We will but not just yet

Godotwait4me: Ok, can I at least tell you my real name?

notall2gether: Deal

Godotwait4me: Blake Harrison

[notall2gether has logged off]

Shut Up!

Dash is too excited to stay still
He bounces around
Like kid on road trip who needs to pee
Now!
I look to Boots as a voice of reason
She strokes my hair and lies
It will be all right

Don't care what world thinks
Sometimes lying is not only okay
It's humane
He only changed his Facebook status to single because he's
*   a private person*
Mrs. Zucker won't fail you; she likes you
That tattoo totally looks real, totally

How Could I Not Have Known?

Yes, we don't run in the same circles
But shouldn't some alarm have been set off?
Warning: nerdy pig about to intercept Greek god in four,
*   three, two . . .*

I Read and Reread

All emails, texts
Never once did he happen to say

Oh, btw, I'm so far outta your league
It's all a farce

Was This All Just a Joke?

Does he know who I am?
Could he be forwarding all my texts to his friends?
Are they sitting at the table reading my emails
In between smoking and skipping class?

Just As They Head Out

They decide to take another look
Here comes their favorite part:
Shay talks about being lonely
What a loser

Shay!!!

I'm about to scold Dash
For pulling me out of my
Rant

Then I See Her

Boots
Has passed out

Nothing Matters
Only her
We pick up cells
Dial numbers and
Pray

For the Next Few Days
Boots lies in ICU (Stupid Name)
It's like the room saying
I See You hurting and
I don't care

Dash and I Decide
We are camping out by her hospital room
If we could do it for Black Eyed Peas show tickets . . .

It Is Days Before
She is allowed out of ICU and can have visitors
Her first question once she comes around?
"Did I miss the *Star Trek* convention?"

Boots Orders Us Not to Worry

She would have had better luck asking us to
Sprout wings and head
South

I Miss Godot

He would understand and care
He'd find a way to make me laugh
And we'd pretend like
All is well

Not Even If We Were the Last

People on earth could I call Blake
Online he's mine
In real world
He belongs to everyone else

She Is Playing

"I'm not as sick as I look"
She's failing
To convince us

> **Godotwait4me:** Are, you ok? Haven't heard from you.

> **Godotwait4me:** What's up? . . .

> **Godotwait4me:** Hello? . . . Hello?

Must Ignore

Must break off all contact
Can't survive him knowing
His cyberprincess is really
Lonely
Pig girl

Let's Dance!

> **Godotwait4me:** Hey, R. Am sending you

> **Godotwait4me:** the new Plain White T's song.

> **Godotwait4me:** Check it out

Don't Do It!

Don't contact him
It's what's best for you
Both
Better hurt now than later

> **Godotwait4me:** Rain, I'm starting to get worried. Did you meet another inbox you like better?

> **Godotwait4me:** What is it? Their font? Their bandwidth? Bc well some guys fake that

> **Godotwait4me:** just to impress a girl.

> **Godotwait4me:** Seriously, hit me back. I miss you

He Wrote For

Days on end
I made myself protect myself
Did nothing

Thing Is

Now I see him
Everywhere
In the chips on my cookies
The steam in my latte
The glaze on my doughnut

Dash Is So Overwhelmed

By Boots's illness
He needs an escape but this time
Golf and tacky patterns
Won't be enough

He Spends a Lot of Time With

Sam
Pretending that he's
Not pretending anymore

When He Lost Interest in Golf
Dad thought tournament was too much pressure
Sam came over with
Gay flag pin
On backpack
Was treated like dog
By Dad
Sam sought distance
Dash sought shelter
The two kissed

Sitting in the Stairwell
Gazing at rows of empty lockers till they blur
I am now six again in car with Dad
Road rolls out like red carpet
We have nothing but time
We snap, sway, swing
"American Pie"
Dad shouts, "I love this song!"
Presses repeat

Now on the Stairwell

The hallways are soundless
Loneliness twists its way
Into my center and
Squeezes
      To stop hurting
      I use voice to bring him back
Singing softly
Dad starts to form before me
By the time I reach the chorus
I am deep in memories
Don't notice
Blake Harrison standing there

Bewildered

Blindsided
Breathless
He calls out
My name
But not my name
"Rain . . . ?"

I RAN

F   A   S   T   E   R

                         T
                         H
                         A

H   U   M   A   N

F   E   E   T

W   E   R   E
                 V
                 E
                 R

M   E   A   N   T
                         O

Cinderella

Slinks out of the ball
So he won't see her rags
Mice. Pumpkins. Back fat.
No glass slippers left to ID her
Only trail of shame

I Know

People my age are always dramatic
Maybe I fall right in line
Judge me later
Answer me now
Has anyone ever died of embarrassment?

By Now

News is all over
Face/Tube/tweet

All Day Dash Has Been

Inspecting classrooms, hallways, entrances, exits
To ensure I don't run
Into Blake
Or
The wave of laughter from White Noise

The Dread

Of running into him
Is second only to the
Hope
Of running into him

It Hits Me Then
Maybe he didn't say anything
To the White Noise
Maybe it was as special to him
As it was to me

Then I Hear the Laughter
Coming down the hallway
The White Noise has gathered around Kelly Canyon's
    locker
Standing right by her side is
Godot Zeus Blake
Whatever you want to call him
He is laughing
With *her* at *me*

You Can All Kiss My . . .
Words
Fly out of me
That I didn't know I knew
        Yes, he fooled me
        Into thinking he liked me
        That was the plan, right?
Get the pig to think she was a real girl?

You Have Been

Chatting with her?
The White Noise asks

They Didn't Know!

They had NO idea
Blake did NOT betray me

But I Just Betrayed Him

Worse
He is bleeding internally
From the vicious words
I chose

Boots Says Slowly

So he actually liked you?
Yeah
And you betrayed him?
Yeah
Embarrassed him in front of entire school?
Yeah
Boots calls for reinforcement

Dash Comes Quickly

Gives me the "You are working my nerves" look
And calls me "destroyer of romance"
(In a loving way)

He Then Announces

He had another encounter w/ Sam
Notebooks touched; sparks flew
A date for the dance was made!

Both Boots and I

Want to ask "What about your dad?"
But there's a rule about stopping Dash mid-dance
Don't. Do. It.

Next Day at School Where

Overripe banana
Gray meat
Warm milk
Mix
     Glam girls. Gym shorts.
     Pain pills. Pop quiz.
Make life hell

When Suddenly, He Speaks to Me

"Hi, Shay"
The tick
Doesn't follow
The tock
Planet stands still

His Words

 Simple, unsophisticated
But bombs
  While
 Simple, unsophisticated
Still blow up

Carnage

From blast spread through White Noise
Leaving mutilated bodies
   A freshman's eyes LEAP!!!! out of sockets
A couple's skin slides off bones
   A senior's jaw drops to basement
A staff's member's ear bleeds rivers

Godot Sees the Remains

Of social convention shatter underneath his feet
    Will he try to
    Reassemble? Mend? Repair?

How???

Maybe he meant different Shay?
        Maybe he's victim of high-fever delirium?
Maybe he is comedian doing routine
"Us"
Punch line

He Looks @ Me

Then slams foot on social convention
Hard.
Grinds it into fine powder
Laughs as it blows away
"Gotta get to class, Shay. Call you later."
Brave.
He's just
Brave.

Like a Fish

Given shoes
I have no idea what to do
            I am scared to look at him
            Scared to look away

At Lunch

Dash recounts his three life-changing moments:
The death of Steve Jobs
His very first Abercrombie & Fitch catalog
And today . . .
When Blake Harrison said hello to Shay Summers!

Send a Quick Mental Tweet

@shayscheeks pls do not blush. pls. pls.
5 sec. later
Blood
Rushes. Races. Runs.
To both cheeks
Next time, I'll send an email

Dash Gushes

"Shay, I'm so in love with your social life
Seriously thinking of being you
For Halloween!"
I Go With A Lie
"It's no big deal"

Dash Treats My Lie

Like rancid meat on five-star menu
"Sorry, boo, we ain't gonna buy that"
I go with a smaller lie
"I mean, it's whatever"

Dash Counters

"*Whatever* is like tofu
You can slice, dice, fry, roast
Grill, glaze
Sauté it
But it's still tofu
And don't nobody want it"
              "What do you want then?"
"The meat, honey: the truth"

Before I Can Answer
He enters.
"Can I sit here?"
Blake Harrison
Just asked to sit next to
ME!
Somewhere pigs have taken flight . . .

Dash Nudges Me
Then he pleads for me to borrow words from him
"No," I protest.
(All his words come dressed in body glitter)

> Need cool, calm reply
> "Whatever" (tofu???)
> I. Am. So. Lame.

He Sits Beside Me
Dash orders mental popcorn
Extra butter
Leans back to watch movie unfold

The Two People in the Film

Don't know their lines
The two people in the film
Dip fries in milk
Drink pizza, eat juice
The two people in the film
Are . . . strangers.

Bell Rings

Film's over; audience leaves
Wants girl recast now
White Noise went from whispers to shouts
"Why is Blake talking to HER?"

Fed Up w/ This, Dash Shakes Me

"Shay, maybe you say something to him . . . it may be
Stupid. Dumb. Uncool.
So what?
Just say SOMETHING!!!"

The Very Next Day

The film has sound!

"Um . . . fries aren't bad," I say.

"Um . . . yeah," he says.

Not Oscar-worthy but still . . .

The White Noise continues to

Cruise. Creep. Crawl.

   Between our eyes

   Between our smiles

   Between our breaths

It seems everyone

Who is anyone

Comes to see the show

Pig Girl

&

the God

Now appearing at Arthur High!

Come one, come all!

Witness a god's downfall!

We Hunters

We hunters grow restless
Have not slept all night
We lay many traps
None of them are right
       We seek footprints
       From a beast that leaves no tracks
       We seek to destroy
       What doesn't fear sword or ax
How do you listen
For prey that makes no sound?
How do you hold and capture
What can't be bound?
       Should this elusive beast appear
       Should it growl in your face
       Beat it, beat it, chain it
       Till it stays in place
Call all the world
Post a sign on your door
Conformity has been caught
Shay outcast no more

School Days Have Been Hell

The eyes. The ears. The lips.
Of White Noise make EVERYTHING awkward
We are fish in school-size bowl

>Which direction will they swim?
>And for how long?
>*Wish we had plastic castle to hide in . . .*

We try to be
Like the rest
I go to his games and cheer loudly!
He reads books I love and cheers loudly!
We meet up by lockers. Classrooms. Hallways.
Anywhere we go
White Noise soon follows

Don't the Eyes Bother You?

I text what I cannot say out loud

Godotwait4me: What eyes?

notall2gether: Um . . . the entire school!!!

Godotwait4me: Don't see them. Don't see anything but you

notall2gether: Sweet. But you can't block out whole school

Godotwait4me: Watch me

The Next Day
Receive text
Ms. Summers, you are invited to tour the world with the
    sender of this text
Along with Godot's message an image is attached
The Eiffel Tower
I smile, thinking
It's a joke
Till he comes alongside me
And whispers
"Bonjour, mademoiselle"
French (even basic)
Very sexy

Last Week
When we were at lunch we went to Cairo
When we were in the halls we rode the gondolas of Venice
When we were in the crosshairs of White Noise
We traveled in our minds
Suddenly, harsh glare of White Noise became radiant glow
A thousand stars

It Isn't Just the Traveling (That I Love)

It's what he shares with me
In Greece he told me about coming home
To find his dad moved out
In Milan he told me about his first pet hamster (Lightning)
Who met an unfortunate end with the neighbors' pet snake
In Hawaii he told me about his latest wet dream
And how I had a starring role
In Ibiza on a rainy afternoon
Under an ivory-colored bridge he told me
He loves me

As for Me?

Atop the tallest skyscraper in Dubai
I told him I still hear
My dad's laughter

In White Sands, New Mexico
I told him about my
"Learn to kiss" pillow

And on a rainy afternoon under an ivory-colored bridge in
    Ibiza
I told him
I love him too

White Noise Surrounds Me

They stop me on the way to
School, class, restroom
"Are You Blake's girl?"
Pretend I'm in a hurry

Till He Overhears One Day

He faces the Noise
"YEAH, SHE'S MY GIRL"

HIS GIRL???

But Girl who gets Boyfriend wears
"Kiss me" lip gloss
"Petite" jeans
"Orgasm" blush

"You Are My Girl, Right?"

He asks when the Noise is gone
Suddenly see secret behind his eyes
OMG!!!
Blake is nervous
"Um . . ."
Don't blow this.
Don't blow this.
Don't blow this.

"Oh, you're not?"

Don't blow this.

Don't blow this.

Don't blow this.

"If you don't wanna be my—"

Don't blow this.

Don't blow this.

Don't blow this.

"Yes! I do!"

OMG, why did I just shout that?

We Laugh

He becomes

Real . . .

Feeling Happy

Like in new soda ad

Like in Disney ending

Like in thin-girl body

Did You Know

Happy people

STILL have

To go to class?

E N T I R E
C l a s s
Is
Fixed
On
Me

Must Have Discovered
One of my
Horrible secrets
Fan letter to cast of
Glee
Squidward-themed desktop wallpaper
Jennifer Love Hewitt playlist.
OMG . . .

The Whispers Begin
When I take my seat
Low humming sends words floating into air
Slowly rising into
Debate. Uproar. Laughter.

Text "911"Godot

Godotwait4me: What's wrong?

notall2gether: News of us hit the entire school

Godotwait4me: Us sounds nice

notall2gether: Focus

Godotwait4me: What's wrong if they know?

notall2gether: They are forming an angry mob

Godotwait4me: Torch wielding or bat swinging?

notall2gether: Torch

Godotwait4me: Great, means they'll come at night. We'll find a place to hide

notall2gether: And regroup

Godotwait4me: Or kiss. Whatever.

notall2gether: Everyone acts so shocked

Godotwait4me: That's what they get for not reading our newsletter "BLA-SHAY" daily

notall2gether: They think I'm not good for you bc . . .

Godotwait4me: Bc?

notall2gether: You know . . .

Godotwait4me: Oh . . . bc you're a lefty?

notall2gether: No . . .

Godotwait4me: Bc you bite your nails?

notall2gether: No :)

Godotwait4me: Bc you freak out when your food touches

notall2gether: Only when it's mash potatoes. And no!

Godotwait4me: Then what?

notall2gether: Bc I'm not . . . thin

Godotwait4me: So what? I like the way you look. A lot.

notall2gether: You're not worried the entire school will laugh at you?

Godotwait4me: No need to worry, if I text you any longer, I'll get kicked out of school

notall2gether: Oh, sorry

Godotwait4me: Who needs education. I can pump gas

notall2gether: I think you need a high school diploma for that too

Godotwait4me: Seriously?

Recap Night w/ Godot with BFFs

Dash warns against a summer wedding
"Sweaty bride is not hot"
Boots pushes for Trekkie theme
Her excitement
Hides shades of blues and grays

"What's Wrong?" We Ask.

"Can I tell you guys something?"
"Anything," Dash reassures.
"I really don't wanna die"
"No one has to know"

We Hold Her

Tighter than a patient should be held
Don't care
Never letting go

Godotwait4me: Heard rents having sex

notall2gether: How did you know?

Godotwait4me: Dirty talk and heavy breathing

notall2gether: How does that go?

Godotwait4me: Heavy breathing? Inhale . . . exhale . . .

notall2gether: No! How do you talk dirty? What do you say?

Godotwait4me: Things like grass stains, mud, grease spot . . .

notall2gether: Haha. For real. Have you tried it?

Godotwait4me: No but doesn't seem hard. You just say "It feels good when you touch that"

notall2gether: What's "that"?

Godotwait4me: Idk, fill in the blank

notall2gether: Ok . . . feels good when you touch my toe

Godotwait4me: Unless you have a thing about feet, that's not really dirty. Pick something else

notall2gether: You go

Godotwait4me: I could say "your boobs feel good"

notall2gether: Who said I would let you touch?

Godotwait4me: You wouldn't let me touch them?

notall2gether: Maybe . . .

Godotwait4me: Lol. Ok, what can I touch?

notall2gether: My heart

Godotwait4me: No fair! That's the hardest part to reach

notall2gether: Not true. You're almost there

Godotwait4me: Then call me Blake

notall2gether: It just seems . . . unreal when I do

Godotwait4me: Ok then, send me pic of your boobs

notall2gether: No ;)

Godotwait4me: Heart or boob.

notall2gether: Hey, um . . . you know I'm not gonna have sex with you right?

Godotwait4me: Wait . . . I'm the one who's not having sex with you. You think a few sexting words and a great date is enough to get me in bed? No way! I need to be wooed . . .

notall2gether: I heard you are easy. Giving it up to students, cashiers . . . the Avon lady

Godotwait4me: That #%#%& promised she'd never tell!

notall2gether: LMAO

Godotwait4me: She offered lifetime supply of mint shampoo. And well, a man has needs.

notall2gether: Was she gentle?

Godotwait4me: Rough. Very rough.

notall2gether: And you liked that?

Godotwait4me: Loved it :)

notall2gether: Lol.

Godotwait4me: But I think it would be better with you

notall2gether: Why?

Godotwait4me: Bc her phone kept ringing.

notall2gether: Avon ladies are in high demand

Godotwait4me: Apparently. Promise you will turn phone off when we do it.

notall2gether: If I'm giving it up, it means we are the last two people on earth. So, my cell won't ring.

Godotwait4me: So . . . no chance at all huh? Damn. After I made a playlist and everything

notall2gether: Who's on it?

Godotwait4me: Stewie Griffin rendition of "I will always love you"

notall2gether: You know the way to a girl's heart

Godotwait4me: Seriously though, I'm cool with your "no sex" thing. No biggie.

notall2gether: You sure?

Godotwait4me: Yeah, no biggie.

notall2gether: K, it's late. Should go to bed

Godotwait4me: Stay

notall2gether: Why?

Godotwait4me: Not ready to let you go

Next Day, Sam Meets Me by My Locker

He looks misplaced
"He's gone," he says
"Who?"
"Dash's dad found out about us.
He took Dash's cell away and sent him
To military school."

213

In Case of Emergency

If your life starts F
                    A
                       L
                          L
                              I
                                   N
                                        G
A   P   A   R   T

Breaking from inside out
Pull all BFFs close and
Brace for impact

That Emergency Procedure

Is where I place my faith
GRAB HOLD OF BFFS BOOTS & DASH
     Ten seconds ago the system went
     d

     o

     w

     n

Dash
Hauled off to
Military school!

Oh No!
Sense

        Any

                Makes

                            Nothing !!!

What???
I mean nothing makes any—ARGH!!!!
You know what I mean

DASH
Turns all my problems to

        Dazzling, sparkly jewels of
        "@$#$#@%#@ 'em
        If they don't like you"
Bedazzles my worries till they shine
Like the star he says
I am

        Pairs my fears with confidence and
        Skinny jeans

215

As Soon As School Ends
Head to Boots
Like mine, all her calls to Dash
Have gone unanswered

Over Next Few Days
Boots and I
Try Dash's mom
She is from the
"Husband knows best" era
Will not help us

Next Day, Find Note in Locker
"GBPB"
       ???   ???   ???

Wrong Locker I'm Guessing
Sigh.
Days are years
Without Dash

Only Bright Spot
Is seeing
Him

Godotwait4me: I know you're down about Dash but how do you feel about Halloween?

notall2gether: As a religion?

Godotwait4me: Lol. No, as a reason to dress crazy and party

notall2gether: I'm for it

Godotwait4me: Hudson's throwing a party after the dance. Wanna go?

notall2gether: Heard about it. Invite only.

Godotwait4me: This invite is not formal enough? Should I send fancy font your way?

notall2gether: Well certainly fancier than Times New Roman. What kind of girl do you think I am?

Godotwait4me: *Shay Summers you are invited to Hudson's Bash with Blake Harrison. Please confirm with smiley face.*

notall2gether: :)))))))

Godotwait4me: For a sec I thought you would turn me down

notall2gether: You picked a good font so . . .

Godotwait4me: Whatever it takes to get the girl

notall2gether: Don't know Hudson well. Is he . . . cool with you and me?

Godotwait4me: Sure, we've been friends since 2nd grade.

notall2gether: Did you guys wrestle and play hide n seek?

Godotwait4me: No, we had pillow fights, did each other's hair, and played spin the bottle.

notall2gether: Heard he uses tongue . . .

Godotwait4me: ARGH!!! Ok. Great. Now the nightmares begin. Seriously, he's cool.

notall2gether: Okay . . .

Godotwait4me: You worry too much about what other people think

notall2gether: I worry just enough

Godotwait4me: What will you go as?

notall2gether: If I don't get math homework done, "failing student"

Godotwait4me: I haven't done my work either. Fail together?

notall2gether: Deal.

Godotwait4me: Last year I dressed up like a Red Bull can

notall2gether: Dash and I went trick or treating last year bc he felt we were never too old for sugar high. He went as Madonna

Godotwait4me: Cool

notall2gether: Post Op.

Godotwait4me: Argh!

notall2gether: I know :)

Godotwait4me: What about you?

notall2gether: I never know what to go as

Godotwait4me: Anyone topless

notall2gether: Lol. My boobs may not be as nice to look at as you think

Godotwait4me: I know your boobs are . . . hot

notall2gether: How?

Godotwait4me: Bc you're hot.

notall2gether: Thx. Hey I saw a few kids wearing buttons at school. Know anything about it?

Godotwait4me: What kind of buttons?

notall2gether: It had letters . . . GPBP. Do you know what that stands for?

Godotwait4me: Idk

notall2gether: Kelly pinned one to her handbag

Godotwait4me: I don't really notice Kelly

notall2gether: Nicest.Thing.You.Said. To.Me.Ever.

Godotwait4me: So now do I get to see them?

notall2gether: No :)

Godotwait4me: Worth a shot

notall2gether: Step Satan went out on a date

Godotwait4me: And you are happy and supportive. Lol

notall2gether: Seriously. How could she?

Godotwait4me: It doesn't mean she didn't love your dad

notall2gether: If she did, she would wait before she dated again

Godotwait4me: How long?

notall2gether: 40 years

Godotwait4me: Sounds reasonable.

notall2gether: Dad loved her. And she just forgot about him

Godotwait4me: I get it, Rain. My dad forgot us. But that is mainly Mom's fault

notall2gether: Is she seeing someone?

Godotwait4me: No, said she will stay single wait for my dad to come around.

notall2gether: That's good

Godotwait4me: Except Dad has not come around at all

notall2gether: There's still time

Godotwait4me: I call Dad. Invite him to my ball games. He always says "Next time." But I still ask

notall2gether: So . . . it's official: Hope=Bad.

Godotwait4me: Yet I still carry some with me . . . for us.

notall2gether: Me too . . .

More and More

G   P   B   P
     Buttons are
     Popping up
     Everywhere

It's Scribbled

On Desks. Notebooks.
Walls. Lockers.
On my locker

Must Focus on Costume Party

Invited by
My boyfriend

Later, Kara Knocks

Places mail on bed
Stack of letters
From

DASH!!!!

Read Them Out Loud

To Boots

Per his request:

The Days and

Nights

Of

Inmate

#253-74

If He Doesn't Kill Me

The whole time I was telling Dad
I am gay
Thought
I'd love to get him in a different tie
One that matches the green of his eyes
If he doesn't kill me

Before the Rage
Of my news
    Before the fire
    From his words
Before the fury
Of his hand on my shoulders
"Shaking me straight"
There was
Sadness . . .

Dad Needed Me
To be someone else
    Tried Failed
    Tried Failed
    Tried Failed
When can I
Stop?

Dad Regrets Having Me
It's in his Breath
It's in his Sigh
It's in his Voice
Regret . . .

Gone

Didn't think he'd send me away
Hate so deep wants me gone
Surely he'll miss
My face
My smile
Me?

Mom Hasn't Been Sleeping

She hugs tight
Too tight
    Dizzy . . .
She makes cookies for the road
     Sweet . . .
Dad says
It's for the best
    Really . . . ?

Military School

Is where Sameness lives
       Art hangs itself
           Expression drinks cyanide
Love leaps off roofs

Didn't Plan to Tell Them About Me
Then one slip
About getting mani-pedi
Seals my fate

The Hands
Jett Holden has hands
Like football fields
And like Dad
He hates me

Jett Looks for Me
Like cats look for mice
Bully looks for gay kid

I've Been
Pulled poked punched by Jett
Says it's my fault
For being gay

Don't Bother to Count the Minutes
There are
>> No clocks
>>> In HELL

Hurricane Jett
Has been raging all day
Knocking down everything in its path
My head. My chest. My legs.

Jett Runs a "Spa"
He treats me
To headfirst
Whirlpool
Commode bath
Free of charge

Not Allowed
Outside contact
Missing my girls
Certain Shay is overreacting and causing drama
Boots turned nurses into Trekkies

Didn't Know

Anger would die
        Hate would soften
                And I'd miss Dad
                Most

But Not Today

Every day mice get eaten
But not this mouse
Not today

Pissed

Have not read one glam mag
Have no access to Twitter
And so no idea what Justin B. is wearing . . .
Argh!!!

As the Mouse Rants

The cat comes over
        Sticks out claws
This mouse has claws today too
        Well manicured and ready to
ATTACK!

We Hit the Floor
Jett and I
He is shocked
I am not playing dead
Shocked I am standing my ground

We Roll on the Floor
His fists make contact
With my face

Jett Calls Me
Every name that
Hurts

I Will Not Back Down
See Dad's face
On Jett
Long to destroy them both
Why? Why
Hurt me?

Jett Holds Down My Face

With his hands
He is irate
Will kill me for sure

Lowers His Face onto Mine

He is going to bite me
        OMG
My pretty, pretty face!!!

His Bite

Is not a bite
        It's a kiss . . .

Jett Takes Off like His Name

When he hears the others come
        They help me up

A Kiss???
It was
Wow . . .

Jett Can't
Look me in the eye
Maybe if he sees me
He'll have to see
Him

We Must

Find way to get BFF back!!!
We need kiss details!

Godotwait4me: Be honest, would you think me less of a man if I failed chem?

notall2gether: Aw . . . I don't think much of you now. Lol

Godotwait4me: The thing you're standing on? My ego. In case you didn't know

notall2gether: Yeah, I knew. Lol. Ok, ok. Why are you failing chem?

Godotwait4me: They insist on the correct answer every time. EVERY TIME

notall2gether: How dare they?

Godotwait4me: Why can't they just be happy I got in the ballpark of the right answer?

notall2gether: Good thing you're not going to be a surgeon. I need you to know exactly where you are operating and not "a ballpark area"

Godotwait4me: You are so picky

notall2gether: Well, I'm dating you so . . .

Godotwait4me: Once again: Ego meet Bruise

notall2gether: Stop stalling and go study

Godotwait4me: Damn you :)

Next Day, in the Hall
Kelly stands with Godot "hair commercial" laughing
The kind of laugh that comes
With hair blowing in the wind
And perfect teeth

Kelly Sees Me
Smiles
Puts arms around Godot and

KISSES HIM!
On the cheek

My mind replays slow motion
Her lips. His cheek. My heart.
Let's not overreact
He loves her!!!

"'Overreacting,' Party of One . . ."

"Right this way, young lady . . .
Tonight's specials:
Smoked almond–crusted paranoia
Sautéed jealousy in a rich envy cream sauce
Pan-seared bruised ego on a bed of fresh misery"

Godotwait4me: Rain?

notall2gether: **What?**

Godotwait4me: Hey!

notall2gether: **Hi.**

Godotwait4me: Impact font. Did I do something?

notall2gether: **Idk, did you?**

Godotwait4me: ???

notall2gether: **Is there something you need to confess?**

Godotwait4me: Um . . . no . . .

notall2gether: Please, your Comic Sans font has guilt all over it

Godotwait4me: WHATEVER

notall2gether: Don't you Matisse ITC me!

Godotwait4me: THEN DON'T IMPACT ME

notall2gether: **I saw what you and Kelly were doing**

Godotwait4me: Not gonna answer till you lighten your font

notall2gether: **Fine . . .** what were you doing with Kelly?

Godotwait4me: Don't you Estrangelo Edessa me. I didn't start this.

notall2gether: What were you doing with Kelly?

Godotwait4me: **AGAIN. DON'T. CARE.FOR.YOUR.FONT.**

notall2gether: *Godot, what were you and Kelly doing?*

Godotwait4me: Don't you even try to hide behind the pleasant slant of French Script MT

notall2gether: *Do you like Kelly?*

Godotwait4me: **NO. She was just asking for my chem notes. Why are you acting so CARACURA**

notall2gether: I Am Not!

Godotwait4me: **Argh!!! I come online to talk to you, and you come at me with Impact (bold no less) for what? Some girl who gave me a peck on the cheek?**

notall2gether: **Why did she do that?**

Godotwait4me: **She left her textbook in class and I found it.**

notall2gether: **Yeah, right.**

Godotwait4me: **You're being so Dissonant. Why can't we just be** Comic Sans **or**

notall2gether: Times New Roman . . . I'm sorry I'm not Standard enough for you. Maybe I'm not meant to be your girl !

Godotwait4me: *Maybe you're right . . .*

[notall2gether has logged off]

[Godotwait4me has logged off]

239

Did Godot and I Just Break Up

No!
Please
No . . . Tide of tears
Brings unwanted things
Swollen eyes exhaustion
Stepmom

Please!   Away
   Stop   Go
     Acting   Now
       Like   Don't
     You   You
    Care   Know
     I

Her Eyes Plead

I'm trying, Shay
Just tell me
What's wrong

I'm Not Trying to Be

A pain
I'm sorry she got stuck
With me
Why pretend it was by choice?

She Spots the Many
Candy wrappers
Sprinkled throughout my room
Sighs

I Gather the Truth Just Above Her Head
Spelling
     Out
         What
            She
               Thinks
                In
                Her
                Heart
                     Kara, you don't even like me

The Tide
Takes back
Its offering

It's Two a.m.
I'm hollowed, gutted
Unable to fill
Head for kitchen's comfort

OMG

Kara stands in front of fridge

Inhaling chocolate pie!

Seriously

Whip cream in hair

Pie crust on chin

Chocolate sprinkles flying

Tears streaming, nose running

Uncontrollably

Um . . . Are You Okay?

Showing concern for her

Feels as unnatural as

Jeans on a chimp

Still . . .

She looks small, lost

       She looks

       Like me . . .

Her Words

Obstructed by pie filling

So she tries again

This time sorrow swallows

Her consonants and vowels

Like the Negotiator

In a bad action flick
I gently take the pie plate out of her hand
Give her a napkin
Sit her down
It is funny
Or would be
Had the weeping
Not sprung from
So deep

I Let Him Down

She confesses
She designated herself
    My guardian
    Not just on paper
She made a promise to Dad's grave
To raise and care for me
    I'm not a fan of capital punishment
    Told her she would not have to
Strap herself down
Inject responsibility obligation
Into her veins

She Cleans Her Face Off

And laughs
The prisoner is rejoicing
At the talk of freedom
From parenthood

You Don't Get It

She says sadly
As she assembles words
I have yet to completely understand
I have liked you since the second we met.

Why?

I'm not granola
     Skinless tofu sun-baked
Will always be
     Deep-fried extra-crispy
     Disgrace

I Never Said That

Kara declares
I remind her how loud
Her actions have spoken

You Can
Yoga yogurt yuck and
Make me meals with
Nasty natural nutritious glop

They Won't Work
Never found
A diet that does

She Smiles and Says
Just want you to eat when you're hungry
Yell when you're mad
Cry when you're sad
You're trying to change me
She replies simply
I'm trying to help you

Least Tell Me
About the boy
Who's making you cry
Her request is denied
Can't talk about the boy
'Cause there is no boy
Not anymore . . .

"Boots, It's Over!"

It takes Boots
Hours to calm me
"Try again with Godot"
she demands

> **notall2gether:** Hello?

> **notall2gether:** Godot?

> **notall2gether:** Hello?

> **notall2gether:** . . .

Send Dad Email

Know he won't get it
Don't care
Need him now

Send Tons of Email

Venting joking
Loving him
Like he was
Here

The Days
Without Godot
Are years

Gore and Blood
Are hot topics
Halloween
In full bloom

Chill in Air
Gray in clouds
Fear in films
Gloom inside

notall2gether: I know you won't reply. I just saw a "man-eating" hot dog cart and thought of you.

notall2gether: Good night Godot . . .

Everything Is So . . .

Black/White

Shay/Pig

School/Home

eat/cry

eat/cry

eat/cry

Godotwait4me: So . . . this man eating hot dog cart . . . had it eaten anyone you know?

notall2gether: Godot!!!

Godotwait4me: Hey . . .

notall2gether: Um . . . um it ate my friend Shay which is fine bc she was kind of . . . crazy. But now she's been replaced by me.

Godotwait4me: Who are you?

notall2gether: Not crazy Shay version 2.0

Godotwait4me: Wow, an upgrade. Cool.

notall2gether: Godot, about last time . . .

Godotwait4me: Yeah?

notall2gether: I know fonts . . . hurt. And I should have just asked you in "standard" Times New Roman.

Godotwait4me: That would have been good. But what would have been better is if you wouldn't ask at all. I don't want Kelly. I want you.

notall2gether: I know. I just can't understand why . . .

Godotwait4me: Bc I have very good taste.

notall2gether: ;)

Godotwait4me: Every time someone says hi to me doesn't mean that I'm leaving you for them, ok?

notall2gether: Yeah

Godotwait4me: I've missed you

notall2gether: Me too. Godot?

Godotwait4me: Yeah?

notall2gether: Overheard Kelly say you've been losing friends bc you're with me.

Godotwait4me: Some, I guess. So what?

notall2gether: If you were with her, you could gain all your friends back. You know be "king & queen" of all things popular

Godotwait4me: Yeah but then I'd have to endure the "Kelly loves Kelly show" and well . . . nothing is worth that

notall2gether: Are you sure? I hear she has great surprise guests

Godotwait4me: Yeah, She, Herself & Her. It's a trio. They come on and sing their big hit "Me, Me, Me"

notall2gether: I heard talk of a monkey

Godotwait4me: Yeah, but he's in the union so, it's hard to get him to do life-threatening tricks

notall2gether: So . . . no Kelly for you?

Godotwait4me: Not a chance

notall2gether: She's pretty . . .

Godotwait4me: And?

notall2gether: :)

Godotwait4me: Don't worry about Kelly or the "friends" I'm losing. Just work on finding your costume for Hudson's Halloween party.

notall2gether: You're really excited about this party thing huh?

Godotwait4me: We've had a party at his house since forever. It never changes. I like that. Since my rents split, very little stays the same so . . .

notall2gether: I get it. Change mostly sucks.

Godotwait4me: Sometimes it can be good. Like if you change your mind about your "I'm not gonna flash" Godot rule. That would be good.

notall2gether: You wish :)

Godotwait4me: All the time. Lol. Good night Rain.

Cell Blares:
In still night sky
Informs me:
One incoming text
It's him again!!!

I'm Wrong :
Sender's number:
Is not known

Text From ???-???-????
http://www.GPBP.com

It Also Kills Cats
If someone makes bowl
     Of reeking rotting fish guts
     And says, hey you, eat up!
You'd know you were bound
For nausea and pain
     Inside lies cruel twisted curiosity
     Makes you wonder
Just how sick can this *really* make me?
So you open and give it a try . . .

Turns Out

Clicking the link is nothing like eating guts

It isn't

F O O L I S H

It isn't

N A U S E A T I N G

It isn't

P A I N F U L

It is

L E T H A L

Welcome to

Get the Pig Back in Its Pen

"Dedicated to protecting natural social order"

May is the big nasty pig you see below. She has broken out of her pen and was stupid enough to start walking amongst humans. Even amongst the king.

The king is too nice to tell her that she smells like a ton of trash. Or that she weighs as much.

But here is your chance to rescue the king from his all-too-kind heart.

SO . . .

Get the Pig Back in Its Pen

Save our royal hottie from swine!!!

G* *A *M *E *S

May Who???

(May has taken a pic w/the king. Just upload your pic to replace her.)

Pig 'n' Pie

(How many pies can you shove down May's throat? Hurry, the clock is ticking!)

Pig 'n a Blanket

(Grab May and wrap her up in a blanket to send her back to the pen. Careful! She won't go without a fight!)

May She RIP

(How will you get rid of May? Embarrass her to death? Send her off a cliff? Or make a mean breakfast? However you do it, do it quick before the king shows up!)

GPS

Have you spotted May with the king?
If so, mark it here on the map!

RAG CHAT

Here you can discuss what awful rag May has on today.
(There are currently 60 users online.)

Petition:

Save the king!

Currently 99 users have signed up.

Join us!!!

"MAY"
Has
My
Face

Please, Please, Please

Don't ask me how I am feeling

Below are letters

Make your own words

ABCDEFGHIJKLMNOPQRSTUVWXYZ

It's Only Been

F   O   U   R

Hours

Can't write yet

Can't think yet

Can't breathe yet

Go away

Why Are You Reading On?

n   o   t   h   i   n   g

h

e

r

e

NO ENTRY

NO ENTRY

yyyyyyyyyyyyyyyyyyyyyyyyyyyyyyyyyyyyyyyyyyyyyy
yyyyyyyyyyyyyyyyyyyyyyyyyyyyyyyyyyyyyyyyyyyyyy
yyyyyyyyyyyyyyyyyyyyyyyyyyyyyyyyyyyyyyyyyyyyyy
yyyyyyyyyyyyyyyyyyyyyyyyyyyyyyyyyyyyyyyyyyyyyy
yyyyyyyyyyyyyyyyyyyyyyyyyyyyyyyyyyyyyyyyyyyyyy
yyyyyyyyyyyyyyyyyyyyyyyyyyyyyyyyyyyyyyyyyyyyyy
yyyyyyyyyyyyyyyyyyyyyyyyyyyyyyyyyyyyyyyyyyyyyy
yyyyyyyyyyyyyyyyyyyyyyyyyyyyyyyyyyyyyyyyyyyyyy
yyyyyyyyyyyyyyyyyyyyyyyyyyyyyyyyyyyyyyyyyyyyyy
yyyyyyyyyyyyyyyyyyyyyyyyyyyyyyyyyyyyyyyyyyyyyy
yyyyyyyyyyyyyyyyyyyyyyyyyyyyyyyyyyyyyyyyyyyyyy
yyyyyyyyyyyyyyyyyyyyyyyyyyyyyyyyyyyyyyyyyyyyyy
yyyyyyyyyyyyyyyyyyyyyyyyyyyyyyyyyyyyyyyyyyyyyy
yyyyyyyyyyyyyyyyyyyyyyyyyyyyyyyyyyyyyyyyyyyyyy
yyyyyyyyyyyyyyyyyyyyyyyyyyyyyyyyyyyyyyyyyyyyyy
yyyyyyyyyyyyyyyyyyyyyyyyyyyyyyyyyyyyyyyyyyyyyy
yyyyyyyyyyyyyyyyyyyyyyyyyyyyyyyyyyyyyyyyyyyyyy
yyyyyyyyyyyyyyyyyyyyyyyyyyyyyyyyyyyyyyyyyyyyyy
yyyyyyyyyyyyyyyyyyyyyyyyyyyyyyyyyyyyyyyyyyyyyy
yyyyyyyyyyyyyyyyyyyyyyyyyyyyyyyyyyyyyyyyyyyyyy
yyyyyyyyyyyyyyyyyyyyyyyyyyyyyyyyyyyyyyyyyyyyyy
yyyyyyyyyyyyyyyyyyyyyyyyyyyyyyyyyyyyyyyyyyyyyy
yyyyyyyyyyyyyyyyyyyyyyyyyyyyyyyyyyyyyyyyyyyyyy
yyyyyyyyyyyyyyyyyyyyyyyyyyyyyyyyyyyyyyyyyyyyyy
yyyyyyyyyyyyyyyyyyyyyyyyyyyyyyyyyyyyyyyyyyyyyy
yyyyyyyyyyyyyyyyyyyyyyyyyyyyyyyyyyyyyyyyyyyyyy
yyyyyyyyyyyyyyyyyyyyyyyyyyyyyyyyyyyyyyyyyyyyyy
yyyyyyyyyyyyyyyyyyyyyyyyyyyyyyyyyyyyyyyyyyyyyy

yyyyyyyyyyyyyyyyyyyyyyyyyyyyyyyyyyyyyyyyyyyyyyyyyy
yyyyyyyyyyyyyyyyyyyyyyyyyyyyyyyyyyyyyyyyyyyyyyyyyy
yyyyyyyyyyyyyyyyyyyyyyyyyyyyyyyyyyyyyyyyyyyyyyyyyy
yyyyyyyyyyyyyyyyyyyyyyyyyyyyyyyyyyyyyyyyyyyyyyyyyy
yyyyyyyyyyyyyyyyyyyyyyyyyyyyyyyyyyyyyyyyyyyyyyyyyy
yyyyyyyyyyyyyyyyyyyyyyyyyyyyyyyyyyyyyyyyyyyyyyyyyy
yyyyyyyyyyyyyyyyyyyyyyyyyyyyyyyyyyyyyyyyyyyyyyyyyy
yyyyyyyyyyyyyyyyyyyyyyyyyyyyyyyyyyyyyyyyyyyyyyyyyy
yyyyyyyyyyyyyyyyyyyyyyyyyyyyyyyyyyyyyyyyyyyyyyyyyy
yyyyyyyyyyyyyyyyyyyyyyyyyyyyyyyyyyyyyyyyyyyyyyyyyy
yyyyyyyyyyyyyyyyyyyyyyyyyyyyyyyyyyyyyyyyyyyyyyyyyy
yyyyyyyyyyyyyyyyyyyyyyyyyyyyyyyyyyyyyyyyyyyyyyyyyy
yyyyyyyyyyyyyyyyyyyyyyyyyyyyyyyyyyyyyyyyyyyyyyyyyy
yyyyyyyyyyyyyyyyyyyyyyyyyyyyyyyyyyyyyyyyyyyyyyyyyy
yyyyyyyyyyyyyyyyyyyyyyyyyyyyyyyyyyyyyyyyyyyyyyyyyy
yyyyyyyyyyyyyyyyyyyyyyyyyyyyyyyyyyyyyyyyyyyyyyyyyy
yyyyyyyyyyyyyyyyyyyyyyyyyyyyyyyyyyyyyyyyyyyyyyyyyy
yyyyyyyyyyyyyyyyyyyyyyyyyyyyyyyyyyyyyyyyyyyyyyyyyy
yyyyyyyyyyyyyyyyyyyyyyyyyyyyyyyyyyyyyyyyyyyyyyyyyy
yyyyyyyyyyyyyyyyyyyyyyyyyyyyyyyyyyyyyyyyyyyyyyyyyy
yyyyyyyyyyyyyyyyyyyyyyyyyyyyyyyyyyyyyyyyyyyyyyyyyy
yyyyyyyyyyyyyyyyyyyyyyyyyyyyyyyyyyyyyyyyyyyyyyyyyy
yyyyyyyyyyyyyyyyyyyyyyyyyyyyyyyyyyyyyyyyyyyyyyyyyy
yyyyyyyyyyyyyyyyyyyyyyyyyyyyyyyyyyyyyyyyyyyyyyyyyy
yyyyyyyyyyyyyyyyyyyyyyyyyyyyyyyyyyyyyyyyyyyyyyyyyy
yyyyyyyyyyyyyyyyyyyyyyyyyyyyyyyyyyyyyyyyyyyyyyyyyy
yyyyyyyyyyyyyyyyyyyyyyyyyyyyyyyyyyyyyyyyyyyyyyyyyy
Me?

Heart Is

Mango tossed in street
        Run over by Mack truck
Split Smashed Veins Valves
        Burst. Splat. Smear.
Step on bits of
Me

How Could I Think

People okay with me w/Blake?
    Come back, little piglet
    Playtime is over

Dealing

Gorged Gooey Greasy Grub
Gonna Get Gargantuan Gut

G   O   O   D

There Was a War

I fought it and lost
Enemy sought win
At any cost

Inhaled burger bombs
Rapid-fire desserts
Promise to love me
Till it no longer hurts
Enemy used propaganda
Everything's a lie
Hurt returns
With the last slice of pie

Salad. Brown rice. Fruit plate.
I could say I win
But I lack will
Yet again

Enemy grins
Its smile greasy
It chuckles
"This is too easy"
It won't make the news
Channel two, five, or four
But here on this very spot
There once was a war

It seems
In the end
Even tears will run out
On you

A Question

Invades mind like termites
             Running inside skull
Eating away all remaining sanity
             Does. He. Know. About. Website?

??

notall2gether: You there?

Godotwait4me: Yeah, just got home.

notall2gether: Did you know?

Godotwait4me: Know what?

notall2gether: About the website

Godotwait4me: . . .

notall2gether: Don't send me any damn dots. ANSWER ME

Godotwait4me: Yeah, I heard about it

notall2gether: Why didn't you tell me?

Godotwait4me: I don't tell you about every awful thing I hear. If there's a three-car pileup with strangers, I won't text you. Why ruin your day over something you can't change?

notall2gether: These aren't strangers. They're kids who hate me

Godotwait4me: %#$@*% them. They don't really know you

notall2gether: It doesn't matter. They want me dead. You knew and didn't say anything

Godotwait4me: I was protecting you. I didn't want you to get hurt.

notall2gether: Then you fail bc this hurts more than I can tell you.

Godotwait4me: I'm sorry.

notall2gether: Before we met only a few kids got on me. Now, I'm being terrorized by the whole school.

Godotwait4me: Hey, they get on me too but I don't care

notall2gether: Who gets on you?

Godotwait4me: It doesn't matter. I just mean that I don't let it get to me.

notall2gether: Who is getting on you about being with me?

Godotwait4me: Hudson. He didn't invite me to his party. But so what?

notall2gether: He's your best friend

Godotwait4me: Guess he wasn't.

notall2gether: Great, that's just great. Now you're losing your BFF? I can't do this anymore. I'm sorry.

[notall2gether has logged off]

Godotwait4me: Shay? Shay?

Will Not Allow
Weeping
Too much of that already
      Fall asleep dreaming
Playing Monopoly
      "Dad, if you let me have ice cream for dinner, I
won't charge you when you land on my property"

Next Day Am Late to Class
Rush to locker
Find note from him

Heart Leaps Into
Throat, hands won't be still
HE says:
Know that "them" is
"They" and "they"
Don't matter
We can turn villagers to believers
Raging voices to melodic song
Flaming pitchforks to soft light
Won't open our doors, minds, hearts

271

Won't invite, entertain, tolerate
Wicked ways
We won't. Let "them" in.
Don't Let Them
We won't. Let "them" in.
Don't Let Them

Tell My Heart

Don't run to him
This is best

Godot Calls

Emails, texts

Won't reply

A Few Days Later

I have ignored Godot
Forty-two times

It's the Hardest Thing

I've done

Kelly Canyon Can't
Stop
Smiling . . .

News of Our Breakup Spreads
Website posts party banner
King Drops Pig!
Yay! Yay! Yay!

A Week Later
Godot
Texts: *Ok. I'm Done*

And So He Is
He makes no more attempts

Boots Is Irate
Since learning about site
        She tried
To escape hospital
        To confront
Kelly Canyon

Orderlies

And guards had to
            Hold her back

She Spits Words

Only formed by
            Tattooed truckers
In bad film

If Dash

Were here
He'd find a way to
            Sparkle this situation

Longing for Dash Gives Way

To anger
Target:
Dash's dad
Fury propels
Me to Dash's
Home
Boots texts me:
Sent you backup
            Got to Dash's house. Found backup warring
            with himself.

274

"Hi, Sam"
"H-h-hey"

> He looked like child on a dare
> Stay the night in the haunted house

Dash's Dad Opens Door
I shoot Word Bullets

"How Dare You?"
Words make contact
With his chest

"She Just Wants to Know Why You Sent Dash Away"
The backup tries to repair damage

"You Are His Dad. Your Job Is to Love Him," I Shoot Again
He stands still
Fearing more will come

> He is right

"It Doesn't Matter"

If he's gay
>If he's a fat left-handed
>Alien

He Clears His Throat in a Dad-Like Manner

"My son is lost. I am helping him find his way back."

The scared kid takes deep breath approaches monster
"Mr. Montgomery, the first time you liked a girl, you knew
    because
Hands sweat. Mouth dries. Heart pounds."
            "So what?" the monster roars
"So, when a boy likes a boy
Hands sweat. Mouth dries. Heart pounds.
It's the same thing," Sam pleads

The Monster Doesn't Agree

"It's not natural," it says.

My Backup Needed Backup

"My dad is gone
I GET NO MORE
Stern talks. Pep talks. Boy talks.

I will never be
Hugged again. Held again. Loved again.

It hurts . . .
When I wake
It hurts . . .
When I sleep

Dad's absence
Acid through heart
Time eats away
Memories

Beg. Plead. Cry.
Nothing brings him back

I'm awake
It hurts again . . .

Dash is feeling the same thing
You are a dad
You have one job
Love your kid.
Mr. Montgomery
Do your damn job!"

I stomp away
Leave him with his shock
And conscience

Did I just . . . ?
I yelled at Dash's dad
A grown man
The size of a tree

A Week Later, Halloween Dance Arrives

I enter
The gym's been transformed
From place where: I get teased
To place where: I get teased
While music plays

     The orange-and-black decorations
     Smoky room, creepy songs
     Make "fear" factor

Just being among crowd
Makes fear a factor
(No need for the sound effects)

I'm Surrounded By
Parade of demons dressed as
Nurses. Princesses. Kittens.

While They're Different Costumes
They wear same mask
They make same adjustment to attire
Now each requires a seedy street corner
To complete the look

In Other Words
They are all
Slutty
The Nurse. The Princess. The Kitten.

All of Their Costumes Are
Too short
Too tight
Too much

The Guys Are All Dressed as Dogs
Even with
Varied costumes
There's
Batman. Sherlock. Cops.

Yet
Trust me
They are all
Dogs
They chase girls
And bark

I Go to the Dance Alone
For the same reason
Pretty blond girls in films
Investigate strange noise in basement —

                                        I'm an idiot.

Seriously, Why
Go to this dance alone?
Knowing I'm AT this dance alone
And how the hell do I
Dance
Alone?

Shay Summers, you promised
You would come to dance
To represent
Others who could not be here

Boots and Dash
Dance for
Them.

Okay, Fine
Will enter
Dance
Alone
And
Dance
Alone

What If
Godot sees me?
I will melt, like
Crayons in microwave
Butter in searing pan
Wicked Witch and water

No! I Will Not
Hide from ex
Will be brave
Visible
Stand my ground

It Just So Happens My Ground
Is near the wall, by the punch bowl
Everyone in
The in-crowd
Stops to note
That
I am here
Alone

They
Whisper. Sneer. Judge.

I don't care
Will stand
Here looking
Unfazed. Uninterested. Unconcerned.

About what THEY think
Ha! Like "they" ever think
They just form

Mobs
Attack
>Well, tonight: I won't be chased off
>Tonight, I will stand
>Still
>For everyone who
>Ran away
>This is my
>Last stand
>Just me, the wall, and the grape-lime punch bowl

There Was a Chance That I Could

Have gone unseen
A chance I could have gotten away with
Very little scarring
But, across the dance floor is
>Kelly and her Pointy Finger of Judgment
>She makes sure everyone
>Knows I'm here
>Alone

I Don't Believe in Violence

But I don't believe
All life is precious
I think Kelly
Should be under bed of earth.

She looks over
To see if I have tears to
Donate to her cause:
"Drive Shay Mad" fund

"Not Today, You Demon Spawn!"
I shout in my head
In real life, I
Smile
Yes, a smile
Is all the
She-beast is getting.

I Never Thought I Would
Feel this emotion at a dance
But here it is: pride!

"Okay, Maybe I Can Do This"
I confirm to myself out loud
Maybe I am stronger than they thought
Maybe I am
Stronger than
I thought . . .

I Start To

Move to music
Sip on punch
Crunch on chips

Look, I'm Fitting In!

What???!!!!

I Smile

Not to prove anything to Kelly
But because I am happy

I'm at a Dance Alone and I Am Okay

Shay Summers is
Okay!!!

"Shay, Hi"

Godot says behind me

I Want to Turn and Face Him

My body has different plans
Make a quick inquiry:

285

Dear Arms and Legs,
This is Shay Summers
Where are you going?

Dear Ms. Summers
Our current destination is:
Away.
We are going away.

I don't remember
Bursting past double doors of gym
Guess I did
As I am, now, outside dance
Shay is outside
While everyone is in
So what else is new?

Never Should Have
Come
Heading now where I
Belong: Boots's bedside
At the hospital
I fill her in on my
Nightmare at the dance
She scolds my frantic run

For the door
I bow my head
And blame my legs

We also lament
Failure to bring
Dash home

Not Sure That's All That Is Upsetting
Boots. She is distant
     Helloooooooo?
She snaps back to the present
"Boots, out w/ it. What's wrong?"

"Shay, I've Been Dying for a Year"
Should be easy now
Her body
Folds under weight
Of fear

Hold Her
Till world ends
Or till she is steady

"It's Okay to Be Afraid"

We're fifteen

Uncertainty is

Our right

"Oh No! Runny Nose, Puffy Eyes: Very Un-Gaga, Ladies"

Turn. Find

Him there

My

Sparkle Dazzle Shiny

DASH!!!

Light Breaks Through

Abyss of weeks gone by

Nurses and doctors

Run in wake of

Our screams

They scold. Use

Words like

Hospital and *policy*

And other words
        We are too loud

We bury him in questions
Says his dad
        Freed him this morning

"And what about Jett?"
"Heartbroken when I left, of course"
        Of course . . .
He's glowing
There'll definitely be emails

"What made your dad change his mind?"
"He's scared of Shay
And something about doing his job?"
Dash asks what it meant

I Smile
And hug him again
        Today something is gonna get bedazzled
"I need a condom"
Boots declares to the room
        It's weird. She used all English words.
        Yet . . . ????
Dash has similar reaction

"Um, come again?" he asks.
Boots tries to sound casual
She fails
She looks around the room
At everything. Everything but us
We wait

"I Want to Have Sex," She Says Yet Again

I want to feel something inside me
Other than tumors
I want to lie down for something
Other than x-rays
I want to lift my shirt for someone
Other than my doctor
I want to cry out from something
Other than pain

Both Dash and I Start Talking at Once

We steal lines from after-school specials
Like wait for the right guy
Like wait till it's special
Like
Wait till you're in love

"WAIT?"

Boots counters using terminally ill logic
Waiting is for people with time
Dying girls only own now
"Stop saying that!"
Dash orders like teacher to bad student
"Divas don't die. You know what?
We need a little Gloria."

NO!!!!

We beg him
But it is too late

> Cue Dash Montgomery's theme song
> ### "At first I was afraid—"

Boots Cuts Him Off Before the Chorus

Don't lie
Thinking it will make me happy
Don't hide
Truth thinking it won't find me
Don't tell
The dying girl she'll be fine
Thinking she'll die slower

I Hold Her Hand
To my chest
"No more talk of death"
I plead

She Confides in Us
My Doctors are soldiers
      In the beginning I was World War II
         Now I am Vietnam

Boots, It's Okay If You Don't See
The love of your life coming for you
I didn't see Godot coming into my world
But he did
(Though it didn't work out . . .)

Dash didn't think his dad would come around
But he did
Why, why can't something AMAZING
Happen for you too?

You think I could find AMAZING?
Despite herself, she smiles
I can't even find my way out of this bed

Dash lights up

Out of this bed? Honey, we can do much better than that

This is bad . . .
        Dash announces
We are going to CRASH Hudson's after party!
Like I said, this is bad.

"WHAT???" Boots asks

I Try to Be
Logical one
        Point out Dash too impulsive
        Boots too sick
Dash pays me no mind
Announces proudly
        "I have the perfect party hair
        For tonight!!!"
Note to self: Logic is useless in face of
Stubborn Trekkie
And boy with extensive
Wig collection
"NO. N-O. NO!"
I protest loudly
        Boots uses her best "sick person" half smile
"NO!"
I remain firm
        Boots tries again

"Shay, I Don't Want . . ."

I don't want my last days to be spent
In this bed in this room
I don't want my last glimpse
To be of me in paper gown
I don't want my last breath to be taken
In a place so filled with last breaths
"Shay, please?"
Damn. Them.

"Okay, Okay!"

Dash says
We will show those
B@$@#$%
        I am still unsure
        Till he reminds me
What I gave up

Have Perfect "Screw 'Em" Costume

Dash lights up
When words
Pass his lips

He Says, "They Think You're a Pig?"
Be MOST
Fab
Pig
Ever!

Miss PIGGY, Baby!

Noooooooo!!!
But the more Dash pushes
The more I
Like it

Boots Sneaks Past
Nurses' station
And heads to
Exit

Meet Up at My House
Dress Boots up as
Mental patient

Dash Dresses Up Like Soldier

Pink fatigues

And lip gloss

He Dresses Me in Bedazzled

Pig snout

Curly tail

Blond ringlets

He Makes a Call

Out in the hallway

Won't let us listen in

Before We Can Object

He rushes us off to

Crash and party

As We Near Hudson's House

It starts

Pain inside chest

Losing Godot

Still hurts

Enter Hudson's Home
"Fairies" "Monsters" "Rappers" "Cops"
Eating. Laughing. Dancing.
All stop

They Look Up As
"Mental Patient" "Soldier" "Piggy"
Enter

Maybe This Is Bad Idea
Dash holds hand tight

The Room Fills With
Laughter. Mocking. Pointing.

Dash Does
Not Care

Boots's Glare
Scares Them

Me?

Yes, I Care . . .

Remember

When I once had Godot
        As a shield
Now I'm defenseless

How Could I

Have given him up?
        How do you hand happiness over?

In His Emails

Texts
Sounded
Lost. Sad. Broken.

Tears. Now???

No No No
        Don't cry
        Here

Too Late
They come slow
But steady

Dash Turns Me
To face staircase

Everyone Watches Him
He Wears
            Green Gloves. Green Makeup. Green Collar.

Godot Is . . .

Kermit!

As he parts crowd
And heads for . . .
Me

I Want to Be Cool, Godot Says
But how could you
Cut me off just like that?
Just like that . . .

I Explain It to Him, Best I Can

Alone and I are old friends

Grew up together

Meet the girl who couldn't outrun

Emptiness out to get her

> She hides secrets behind her eyes

> And hopes her tears won't give her away

Godot Reveals

Alone and I are old friends

Grew up together

Meet the boy "trending" and "accepted"

Who doesn't care to be either

He Wants Her to Know

It's okay

To not be okay

It's all right

To not be all right

> He wants her to know

> He loves places where she is fractured

> Gaps in confidence cracks in her armor

He wants her to know

It's okay if she's broken

'Cause he's broken too

He wants her to know
The one who gets overlooked
Is the only one he sees

I Wonder

Could Godot really be
My Romeo Tristan Edward
Even if I am not
Juliet Isolde Bella
Beautiful?

Godot, Girls Like Me —

He stops me midsentence
His fingers on my lips
His fingers . . .
My lips . . .

Shay, There Are

NO girls
Like
You

He Extends His Hand
Asks if I'd like to dance
He asked ME!
Shay Summers . . .

I Swallow
Hard and confess
"I DON'T OWN ANY SKINNY JEANS!"

He Beams
One less article of clothing
To try and get you out of
        I laugh
        He brushes my cheek
        With warm hands

So . . . You Wanna Dance?
He asks again

Miss Piggy, Would You Like to Dance?
Can't Find Words
Where

Did

        I

                Misplace

Them

        Damn it!!!

Just Nod, Shay . . .

We head to dance floor

I'm floating

        In arms of frog

Everyone

Is too stunned

        To move

Crowd Fades

From mind

        Only us

Us . . .

The Poet

Uses words because

She never learned how to
Apply makeup
And now she is
Out of words . . .

Defenseless, Huh? Godot Says

Then smiles, whispers
> You can lower armor
> You can drop shield
> You can be here

Here

Where weapons
Aren't needed

> ## "Godot, I'm—"
> My name is Blake.
> Not Godot.
> Not Kermit.
> BLAKE.

Hi, Blake

Hi, Shay

Dash Explains That He Called ~~Godot~~ Blake

    And told him

    Why I

    Let him go

Blake Says He Doesn't Want

    Them

    He

    Wants

    Me

I Ask a Very Important Question

"So, Blake, how do you feel about turkey bacon?"

We laugh.

"So . . . you really like me, huh?" I say.

"No, Ms. Piggy. I love you. You get that?"

"Yeah, I think I *finally* got it . . ."

It's Just That for So Long . . .

He doesn't let me finish

His kiss

Stops

E V E R Y T H I N G

Hudson Comes Over

The two stare
Each other down
     Midnight
      In bad gunslinger flick

Hudson Turns to Me

"Blake says you're funny. Say something funny"
"Funnier than your haircut?"
"Unnecessary roughness . . . I like that"

Blake, We Good?

Hudson
Waits . . .

He Admits

No invite was
Kelly's idea

Something in Me

       Has Had Enough

I March Up to the Canyon
She looks like gator
After swallowing live prey whole
      "What is your problem with me?"
The music stops
No one
Dances. Moves. Breathes.

"Excuse Me?" She Says Innocently
"Why are you always on me, Kelly? What's your problem?"
Pause
Pause
Pause

"You're a Fat Loser Who Doesn't Deserve Anything"
There.
Plain. Simple.
Black. White.
"Got it, piggy?"

Fearlessly

I stare
Into the Void
That is Kelly
And say

"Maybe We Are All Animals . . .

And maybe I eat too much
But better a pig
Than a
Bitch"

I Hear Laughter

As the Void stands in shock
Blake reaches for my hand
Blake: Miss Piggy, shall we?
Shay: Yes, Kermit.
          We head back to the dance floor.

"You Were Wrong to Go Along, Hudson"

        "Yeah, I know. My bad"
"Whatever, man"
        "C'mon . . . what do you want, tears?"
"Yeah, and maybe a serenade or two"

They Exchange a Look
Friendship intact
Hudson walks away

Some Still Whisper About Us
Blake and I
Too in love
           To care

Slowly Shock
Wears off crowd
Dance music comes on
      Dave Cutter smiles at Boots
      From across the room
      Boots whispers
"Tonight, Dave may go where
No man has gone before"
      We laugh while
      She heads for Dave
Dash eyes Sam dressed as
Human "bedazzle" machine
      They exchange
      Suggestive smiles
Blake and I
Go back to dancing

And Just for a Moment

The Pig and the Frog
Blend in